I0538290

Dimensional Abscesses

edited by

Jeffrey A. Hite

&

Michell Plested

www.evilalteregopress.wordpress.com

Evil Alter-Ego Press

www.evilalteregopress.wordpress.com

Published by Evil Alter Ego Press

869 Citadel Drive NW

Calgary, AB T3G 4B8

Canada

Dimensional Abscesses, Copyright © 2015 by Jeffrey A. Hite and Michell Plested.

Edited by Jeffrey A. Hite and Michell Plested.

Cover by Jeff Minkevics, copyright © 2015 by Jeff Minkevics.

Special thanks to Julayne Hughes for final, polishing edits.

All rights reserved. Without limiting the rights under copyright reserved above, no part of this publication may be reproduced, stored in or introduced into a retrieval system, or transmitted in any form or by any means (electronic, mechanical, photocopying, recording or otherwise), without the prior written permission of both the copyright owner and the publisher of the book.

Publisher's note: This book is a work of fiction. Names, characters, places, and incidents either are the products of the author's imagination or are used fictitiously, and any resemblance to actual persons living or dead, events, or locales is entirely coincidental.

Print version set in Cambria; titles in Cambria, byline in Cambria.

Published in Canada

Library and Archives Canada Cataloguing in Publication

Hite, Jeffrey A.

Dimensional abscesses / Jeffrey A. Hite and Michell Plested.

Electronic monograph issued in EPUB format.

ISBN 978-0-9947266-0-5 (pbk)
ISBN 978-0-9947266-1-2 (epub).

Contents

Introduction

by Jeffrey Hite

What do Sliders, *Dr Who*, *Quantum Leap*, and a hole in my kitchen ceiling have to do with each other? Well, normally I would say nothing, but when you add just one more ingredient – a twitter conversation between my alter ego Michell Plested and me – you get an idea about portals to places that you may or may not want to visit. And, like the characters in the shows, sometimes all you want to do is get home.

No, really, that is how it happened. One night, shortly after Michell and I had finished our last anthology, *A Method to the Madness: A Guide to the Super Evil*, I remarked that we'd had some water damage and that now there was this rather large hole in my kitchen ceiling. Of course, knowing the two of us, you can probably guess what happened next.

Michell: "What is right above your kitchen that leaked?"

Jeff: "The master bathroom. A pipe burst under our sink."

Michell: "So it is like a portal to your master bathroom?"

Jeff: "Technically, it leads to the cabinet under the sink in our master bathroom, but yeah."

Michell: "Well, that is someplace you don't really want to end up."

Jeff: "You can say that again; giant dust bunnies galore."

Or something like that.

And so the idea was born, and with it a new journey.

Obviously, Michell and I have worked together before.

And last time it was a very rewarding experience for me. Since he didn't stop talking to me as soon as *A Method to the Madness* was published, I figured I should take that as a good thing and run with it.

This new book is, I hope, the first in a long line of books that Michell and I will get to work on. With *Dimensional Abscesses*, we also started our own publishing imprint that we are calling Evil Alter Ego Press. We are just getting started on this new endeavor, and while it might be a portal to a place that neither of us know, I think we are going to like it when we get there.

Now, as for *Dimensional Abscesses*, it has been a lot of fun to work with. First of all, how often do you get to travel to so many alternate dimensions, odd places, the past, the future, and other places that you may or may not get to know along the way, virtually for free? All I had to do was read the stories. Second, I got to come back alive, which is more than I can say for some of the characters. I count that as good thing.

Notice that I didn't say unchanged. This is because, just like the characters in these stories, the places we visit in these stories change us. That is what a good story does for you. It takes you to another place; wraps you in the story right along with the character. So when I read these stories, I laughed, and I cried, and I lived right along with the characters, and just like them, I came away changed. That is my hope for you as well.

This book has been a ton of fun to work on. A lot of long hours and hard work went into it by Michell and me and especially the various authors. But, in my humble opinion, it has been completely worth it, because the end product is something that I am very proud of. I hope that you enjoy *Dimensional Abscesses: Stories of Places You Don't Want to Go* as much as I have.

Jeff Hite

Introduction

by Michell Plested

Stories and ideas for stories come from everywhere. Anthology ideas are no different. Therefore, it should come as no surprise when I tell you that the idea for this anthology came from a conversation on Twitter between me and my #EvilAlterEgo, Jeffrey Hite.

Jeff was telling me about how a pipe burst in his upstairs bathroom, which resulted in a hole in the ceiling of his kitchen. When I asked him where the hole in his bathroom went (this was after the conversation had been going on for a while), Jeff likely rolled his eyes before responding that it went to the kitchen.

"But, where does it go from the kitchen side?" I asked innocently. "Perhaps it leads to someplace other than your bathroom."

And from there came the idea of a portals anthology.

Initially, we talked about portals in general, but it occurred to us that not just any portals would do. For example, stories already exist where portals take you through a wardrobe to a fantastic magical realm ruled by a large, benevolent lion. Clearly a place many of us would like to travel to.

But what if the portal stories we focused on lead to places no one in their right mind would want to go to?

Jeff and I had already edited one anthology together by this point (*A Method to the Madness: A Guide to the Super Evil* available from Five Rivers Publishing) and it was a fun challenge. We decided maybe the world was ready for another odd anthology.

Our original title was *Portal Under My Sink - and Other*

Stories of Magical Places You Likely Don't Want to Go; a bit of a mouthful, I'm sure you will agree. What we settled on was shorter and encompassed more than just the fantasy genre: *Dimensional Abscesses* with the tagline, *A Collection of Stories About Places You Don't Want to Go.*

Not satisfied with the simple challenge of producing an anthology for another press like the last one, we decided to fund this one ourselves under the brand-new imprint, Evil Alter Ego Press. This book represents an entirely new chapter in our writing/editing professional lives.

We have brought together ten stories, sometimes fun, often dark, about portals that lead to places no sane person would willingly travel to. Thank you for making the investment of your time to read our anthology.

Michell Plested

Paradise Out of Order

by Kevin Wohler

The relics in Malcolm's shop hummed with power that only he could hear. When he entered the back door each morning, he felt the items before he saw them. Even before the fluorescent bulbs in the ceiling flickered on, each token buzzed to life with power.

As he did on the first of every month, Mal performed an inventory of the items on display in the shop, from books to gems to ingredients. As the only true magic shop in the city, he had a steady stream of regular customers who appreciated the value of what he sold. He also had the occasional visitor who tried to steal him blind — teen shoplifters looking for a thrill or religious zealots trying to do "God's work." If only they understood the danger.

Mal walked past the counter and the cash register to the front door. He unlocked the door and pushed the button that lifted the security gate. He whispered a small incantation, then picked up a black rune stone — the real security measure — propped beside the door.

Outside, a light rain fell on the street. Foot traffic passed by at a quick clip as pedestrians moved to escape the weather. Mal watched for a moment to see if anyone would come down the steps to his door. Once a month, Crazy Mary would come in for supplies, and she'd end up hanging around most of the morning, talking about everything from aliens to Isis to John Denver. The rain would keep her home today, though. He felt thankful for the reprieve.

Mal walked through the shop, taking note of low inventory. Now and then, he'd stop to examine an item dripping with residual power. Some drew power from other nearby relics and needed constant attention. Organizing the feng shui in the shop could be a full-time job.

A box of quartz crystals was draining a set of hand-carved fetishes of their power. Mal replaced the crystals with a jar of sand, collected from the desert under the light of a full moon. Having done so, he felt the carved fetishes begin to recharge.

Before he could finish the inventory, Mal was interrupted by his first customer of the day. A young man, no more than nineteen, entered. His head, uncovered, dripped with rain. The light jacket he wore appeared to keep the water off him, but Mal thought it looked too thin for the cold October morning.

The teen shook visibly, his hand still on the door. "Is this really a magic shop?"

Mal, never one for signs or advertising, had relied on word of mouth to reach potential customers. Besides, a sign that advertised a magic shop would only attract people looking for linking rings and card tricks.

"The Village Alchemist, Malcolm Ward, proprietor." With a flourish, he produced a business card as if from thin air and handed it to the young man.

When he reached for the card, the teen relinquished his hold on the door and stepped inside. The door closed behind him, shutting out the weather. "Is this for real?"

"Is anything?" asked Mal. The philosophical quip was lost on his customer. When he didn't receive a response, Mal continued. "But to answer your question, yes. Real magic. Not illusions. You won't see Penn & Teller in here."

"I need help. I met a guy last night who said you might be

able to help me."

"We don't have love potions or ground rhinoceros horn. If you want that kind of stuff, you'll have to go to Chinatown. Besides, it's all crap."

"No, nothing like that. I was told you have a door."

Mal stopped. "I've got a few. You just came through one. And if you're asking about what I think you're asking, you can use that same door on your way out."

"You have a portal, a Paradisus portal. I need to use it."

"You can't. It's..." Mal paused to choose his next words carefully. "It's not working."

A look of confusion crossed the young man's face. He tensed, as if every muscle in his body had seized up. He banged his fist against a display in the middle of the room. The items on the shelves danced from the impact.

Louder, the kid said, "I was told it could take me to my heart's desire."

"You have outdated information," said Mal. He walked to the back of the store, positioning himself behind the cash register.

Beneath the counter, he kept a variety of personal security items, the least of which was a sawed-off 12-gauge shotgun. Just for emergencies. He didn't think the kid would be a problem, but he didn't like customers who were... insistent. People who wouldn't take no for an answer tended to make poor life choices.

"Sammy said you could help me," said the kid. He had followed Mal to the back of the store but kept a respectful distance.

Mal thought of all his regulars and couldn't imagine who Sammy might be. Second-hand information, no doubt. A friend of a friend. "Sorry, uh..."

"Russell. My name's... Russell."

"Look, Russell. Paradisus portals are rare enchantments. Even more rare when they have enough mojo to work. These kinds of objects need a steady stream of energy — pure energy — to keep from turning sour. That's why they usually exist only in nature. You might find one in a pristine forest or in the middle of a desert where no human has set foot in a thousand years. Sometimes they exist where several ley lines cross, using the Earth's own energy to power them. They're getting harder and harder to find."

"But you have one, don't you?"

"Had. Past tense. Like I said, it takes a steady stream of energy to power them. Without it, the enchantment goes bad and the portal goes...*out of order.*"

The kid looked upset, frustrated, but more than anything he looked heartbroken. Mal expected the kid to lash out at any second and start tearing up the joint. The last thing he imagined was Russell falling to his knees and crying.

Mal rounded the counter and knelt beside him. The kid's tears were lost on his rain-soaked face, but the redness in his eyes suggested this wasn't his first breakdown of the morning.

"Hang on, hang on," said Mal. He tentatively put a hand on Russell's shoulder and gave it a small squeeze. "Whatever it is, it's going to be all right. Maybe we can find another way."

"I can't. It won't. I've been looking for something for weeks now. Asking around." Russell wiped his face with the sleeve of his coat. "Finally met some guy who knew a guy. He said if I gave him a thousand bucks, he could get me the answer."

Mal's stomach clenched as he thought of some scumbag preying on this kid's misfortune. A thousand bucks for bad information. "He was conning you, kid."

Mal pulled Russell to his feet and helped him onto a nearby reading chair. "Besides, a Paradisus portal can't solve problems. It can only take you places. Sometimes running away seems like an answer, but it rarely is."

"I'm not running away," said Russell. "I'm trying to save her life."

Mal didn't react right away. He had heard his share of hyperbole from desperate and — frankly — weird customers. Crazy Mary, for instance, repeatedly insisted that ancient aliens who seeded our planet were communicating through her bedside Shrine of Isis and John Denver.

Something in the kid's voice, however, made him think this wasn't a lovesick teenager being all emo.

"Okay, you have my attention. Who is *she*?"

"My fiancée, Claire. She died a few weeks ago."

Mal processed this new information, trying to decide if the time frame or her death was the more relevant piece of information. He let it slide and said, "Go on."

Russell leaned forward in the chair, resting his head in his hands. "We were supposed to go to dinner. I was running late, as usual, so Claire said she'd meet me at the restaurant. Her car got t-boned at an intersection a block from the restaurant. They said she died at the scene. If I had been on time, I would have been with her in the car."

"And you'd be dead, too." Mal didn't think that was the kid's intention. He seemed lost, not suicidal.

"I heard this portal can take you where you most want to go. I hoped it would take me back, before she got into the car. If I could drive us to the restaurant, maybe take a different route, she wouldn't die."

"Yeah, I can see your dilemma. But newsflash, kid, I don't even know if a Paradisus portal works like that. It's a doorway, not a time machine. At least, I've never heard of it doing that."

"You could try," he said. "I'll give you whatever you want."

The kid reached into his jacket and pulled out a wad of bills that looked like he had nickel-and-dimed everyone who owed him. He probably hocked everything he had of value, too.

"It's all I could scrape together. Take it. It's yours." He let the bills fall to the ground. Mal eyed them and estimated it was somewhere south of $350.

"You're forgetting one thing. The portal isn't working."

"So? I can try. What's the worst that could happen?" Russell stood and started to pace, like a tiger in a cage.

Mal had seen this move before. He called it the *next hit shuffle*. Addicts of any sort got twitchy when they could feel their next hit was close at hand. He had seen it in his brother, Walter, when he was using. He had also seen it in some of his customers when they were buying magic items.

"I don't know what would happen," said Mal. "You might walk through and still be here in the shop. That's the best-case scenario. Worst case, you might end up dead. I know from experience that enchantments tend to go very wrong when they sour."

"There's no way to fix it?"

"If I could, I would have done it by now. I used to make half a million a year on that portal. People would come in and drop down huge sums of money for the chance to find paradise. And in all those years, I never heard a complaint."

Mal sat on the edge of the chair the kid had vacated. "The last time the portal was used, something went...wrong."

Russell stopped pacing and leaned against the counter. His eyes locked on Mal, but he seemed to be thinking about something else. "You made a mistake?"

"It was no mistake. Well, maybe it was. I shouldn't have let the Russian go through. I just wanted to get rid of him. He was a total asshole, a dirt bag, high on something. My guess? Drugs or dark magic."

"He treated his girlfriend like trash — called her every name in the book, with her standing right there. Said he wanted to go somewhere, anywhere, and leave her behind. Honestly, I thought she'd be better off without him."

"After trashing half my store and threatening to kill anyone I ever knew, he demanded that I show him the portal. He also offered me twenty grand in cash to pay for the mess he made, so I agreed."

"From the moment the Russian touched it, something wasn't right. I could feel it. When the portal opened, the air inside was dark and thick, like tar. Something reached out of that gunk and grabbed him, pulled him in. You could probably hear his screams a block away. I hope the bastard suffered."

"Since then, I've kept the portal closed."

"Then how do you know it's not working right?"

Mal didn't know what to tell the kid. He didn't want to encourage him, but he didn't want to lie either. The truth is, he had just known — the way he knew the fetishes were being drained by the quartz crystals. He had a sixth sense about these things.

"I guess you'd have to say it's magic," said Mal. "I'm attuned to the items in my shop and I know things about them."

Russell was quiet a long time, but Mal knew what the next question would be. It was the same question they all asked. Every time he told the story.

"Can I see it?"

"No," said Mal. He turned away and walked toward the front of the store, hoping the kid would follow. "There's no point. You're not going through."

The next thing Mal heard was the sound of a pump-action shotgun — his shotgun — being cycled. He turned and saw Russell standing behind the counter, the gun pointed directly at him.

"I didn't want to do this, but you've left me no choice."

Mal didn't even blink. He didn't want to make matters worse by trying to outthink or outmaneuver his opponent. This was no different than any other hold-up, and he'd gladly empty his own cash register if it meant getting out of the situation without getting shot. Only idiots tried to be heroes.

"Okay, kid. If you want to try to go through the door, I'll let you go. But you've been warned." Mal walked past the counter to the back room, leading the kid with the shotgun.

The storage room was nearly empty; Mal didn't believe in keeping a lot of surplus inventory. Everything he had was in the front of the shop, available for sale. His mind ticked off items as he passed the shelves, hoping there might be something he could use to protect himself in case the kid got trigger-happy. The only objects in storage were a few specialty items he had ordered for customers who never picked them up. Things no one really wanted. He had a few customized tarot decks, a tribal mask from Africa, and a few ingredients from the Amazon. Trinkets more than artifacts. Nothing with any real power.

But at the far end of the small room stood a wooden door

in a frame. The only thing remarkable about it was the fact that it wasn't set into a wall. It stood alone, untouched on any side. The wood was unpainted, but weathered. The frame appeared to be constructed of the same wood, and showed similar signs of being worn by time. Mal wondered offhand if maybe he should sand it down and give it a good coat of varnish.

"Here you go, kid. One genuine Paradisus portal. Normally, I'd give you the sales pitch, but you already know what it's supposed to do. More likely than not, you'll end up in hell."

"I'm already in hell," said Russell. He moved to the door and reached out with one hand to touch it. "It doesn't feel magical."

"The door isn't magic. It's what the door contains. All you have to do is put your hand on the knob, think about what you want, and open it. If it works, you'll be transported to your heart's desire. If not..." He let his voice trail off.

"It'll work," said Russell. "It has to. And if it doesn't, it won't matter. I can't live without Claire."

Mal reached out, then recoiled his arm when the kid turned the shotgun to face him.

"Look, I don't know you and you don't know me. But I can tell you straight up that if she loved you as much as you love her, she wouldn't want you to throw your life away."

"You don't get it. She died because of me." Russell set the shotgun on the floor and kicked it out of reach. Then he took a deep breath, grabbed the doorknob, and closed his eyes.

Mal felt the change before he could see it. The portal purred to life, as energy passed from the kid into the door. He expected to see the same blackness that had enveloped its last victim, but he saw something else — pure and white. Before he could react, Russell stepped forward into the light.

For a moment, the portal stayed open. Mal watched as Russell stepped onto a busy sidewalk. The sun shone down on a cloudless morning — or was it afternoon? The kid looked up the street, then did something unexpected. He stepped directly in front of a car, his hands outstretched. The car skidded to a halt, the bumper missing him by inches.

"Are you insane?" A young woman with long, blonde hair jumped out of the car. "I could have killed you, Russell!"

Mal smiled to himself, knowing she was okay. Angry as she was, she was alive. That was what that mattered.

The portal began to close, but not before Mal heard the sound of squealing tires, followed by smashing glass and bending metal. For a moment he thought he saw a truck, then the view was gone. He saw nothing but the back wall of the storeroom.

Mal reached out and gingerly laid his hand on the door, making sure not to touch the knob. The wood was warm, like a living thing. He listened for the pulse of the artifact and heard a strong, steady beat of power.

"Nice to have you back." He closed the door and patted the frame. "From now on, no more asshole Russians. I promise."

From the front of the shop came the sound of a door opening. Mal had never been the type of shopkeeper to have a bell on the door. He knew when people entered his domain.

"Be right out!" he said, just loud enough to be heard. Mal emerged from the storeroom a moment later. He immediately went to work picking up the loose bills the kid had scattered on the floor.

A young girl approached him, her long, blonde hair soaked by the rain. Through the raindrops on her face, he could see tears. She had been crying.

"Is this really a magic shop?" she asked. "My name is Claire, and a friend said you could help me."

We'll Leave the Lights On for You

by Philip 'Norvaljoe' Carroll

Emit snuggled among his brothers and sisters, happy to be warm and moist and safely squeezed inside the wall beneath the sink. Someone pulled on one of his legs, and though he tried to shake free, whoever did it was more persistent than he was resistant.

Giles. He should have known.

He followed his good friend from the comfortable nest and through a crack between boards. Beneath the sink the smells of mildew and rot reminded him how hungry he was. He peeked between bottles and boxes to see if there was anything new to eat.

"Emit, have you seen the motel? Something's going on there," Giles whispered to his friend.

"Dude. I just woke up. I haven't been anywhere. What do you mean, going on?"

"It's like, there are lights coming out of it. Not like the lights are just on, but like they're moving around, or someone's moving around in there."

"Come on. No one's gone in there since they put the thing up. It's so dusty I have to bathe if I just pass near the place."

Emit shuddered and ran an antenna through his mouth as if to prove the point.

"I know. Me too, but," Giles said and skittered in a circle, "I think we should go check it out. I wouldn't want any of the nits to stumble in there. The place is old and there might still be something dangerous."

Emit laughed. "Don't tell me you're worried about the little ones. I've known you my whole life. You just want excitement."

"Yeah. Okay, well. This is exciting. I think there's a magic portal in the motel."

Emit waggled his antennae. "You've been listening to those old storytellers too much."

They squeezed past a bottle of dishwashing liquid, around some moldy sponges, and there it was, like a rainbow trapped in a matchbox.

Emit looked behind him. "Stop pushing. Dude! You're breathing up my cerci. How am I supposed to tell if someone's sneaking up on us with your humidity all over my butt?"

"I'm just trying to see," Giles whined.

"You've seen it already. Give me some room."

They crouched at the edge of the roach motel; a small rectangular box, open at the near and far ends. Poisoned glue strips on the floor and ceiling of the motel were intended to trap creatures that hid in it when the cupboard doors were opened. The far end of the cardboard tunnel swirled and shimmered with myriad kaleidoscope colors.

"Don't you think it's beautiful?" Giles asked.

"Yeah. But is it safe?" Emit waved his antennae into the box and cleaned them again before he crept around it and back to where Giles waited. "I don't smell any poison and the glue looks so caked with dust, I don't think anyone would stick to it."

"So. Are you going in there with me?" Giles asked.

"Why would you want to do that?"

"Come on. It could take us to someplace really cool, and I don't want to go alone."

"I'm happy right here," Emit said.

Giles crept into the box. "One old cruster told me there's a world out there where the cockroaches rule; where the humans burned themselves to ashes and just left it for guys like you and me."

"Sounds wonderful, but Sylvia finally seems to be warming up to me, and, you know, I'd like to start an egg sac while I'm young enough to enjoy the little nits."

"Think about it, Emit. If you go with me to a whole bunch of strange places and come back to tell Sylvia about them, you'll have her eating out of your hand, dying for you to start that egg sac with her."

"It's the *if I make it back* part that concerns me," Emit said. He drew in a deep breath and exhaled, flattening himself onto the floor as he thought. "Yeah. Okay. If you make it through without getting stuck to the glue board or ending up on your back with your feet in the air, then I'll follow."

"Cool," Giles said, and inched toward the swirling incandescence. He reached forward, passed his antennae through the portal and pulled them back quickly, giggling. "It tickles."

A second later, he was gone.

Emit sighed and followed. He tested the swirling portal with his antennae. It was cool and inviting and he laughed when his whole body tingled, passing through the membrane.

"Goback, goback, goback, goback," Giles was screaming as Emit came fully through the portal.

Emit was one roach who had always been proud of his ability to change directions in the smallest fraction of a second, but even he wasn't fast enough to turn back through the portal before it winked out of existence.

"Oh, dude," Giles cried and danced on all six legs.

What's that sound? Emit thought. The ground shook beneath his feet. The rumble and rush of wind came at them from all directions. Giles had always been adventurous and cavalier but at that moment it was clear he was scared out of his exoskeleton. A giant cylinder rolled toward them, large enough to crush their entire nest. No. Large enough to crush the sink and everything under it.

Emit couldn't remember the last time he was out-of-doors during the day, and the thought that other predators might be able to see him didn't really cross his mind. Spiders, birds, or monkeys were the last things on his mind with this machine threatening to roll him flat.

Giles screamed and Emit turned to see another one of the monstrous machines rolling their direction, a column of white and silver steam billowing above.

"Run, Giles," Emit shouted and took off, running ahead of the machine closest to the two roaches.

Giles was at his shoulder, gasping, "Where can we go? These things are everywhere."

"Nowhere," Emit said.

"Nowhere? What?"

"Just shut up and keep running. I need a minute to think."

Wherever Emit looked, the ground was perfectly flat as if these rolling, flattening machines had done nothing else since the beginning of time.

"This looks more like cockroach hell than paradise to me," Emit said. "How do you think we can get out of here?"

"I don't know. Maybe if we follow these things, they'll take us somewhere better," Giles suggested.

"I wish I'd thought of that," Emit said. "Come on."

The two roaches dashed to the side, around the rumbling monster, and pulled quickly in, behind the steamroller. Following close behind the deep treads of the rear pneumatic tires, they defied death beneath the rollers of other machines by staying in the short wake of safety behind their guide.

Hours later, as the sun began to set, Emit had still not found a pattern or purpose to the steamroller's direction of travel.

"Have you come up with anything yet?" Giles asked. "I'm getting thirsty."

Emit chirped in annoyance. "You should be able to go a week without a drink. What were you doing for the last few days under the sink?"

Giles' reply was drowned out by the grinding of gears and the rattle of loose metal frames as the steamrollers shuddered to a unified stop. With a great rumble all of the machines turned toward the setting sun and rolled away.

The two roaches dodged and danced their way through the herd until the machines rolled from their limited field of vision.

Emit took advantage of the steamrollers' departure and cleaned his antennae. A waxy coating on the exoskeleton was good for keeping moisture in the body, but could play havoc with being aware of his surroundings when the wax got onto his antennae.

"Where do you think they all went?" Giles asked.

"Do you care?" Emit snapped at his friend, waving his antennae in the air. "I realize this is a wonderful adventure for you and your magic portal. But, in case you don't remember, the one we came through is gone. For all we know, we're trapped in this world of killer machines with no way home. Maybe if we can find another magic portal we can move on to your cockroach paradise."

Emit turned and hurried away.

"Where are you going?" Giles called after his friend.

Emit stopped and hissed. "I don't know, poison it all. But those crazy machines went that way, I'm going the direct opposite."

"Can I come with you?"

The poor bug sounded so forlorn it defused Emit's anger and he crept back to his friend.

"Yeah. Come on. Let's see what we can find this way," Emit said, and waited for Giles to catch up. "If we can find a house, maybe there'll be some pretty females to nest down with."

They headed east and crept off across the darkening plain.

"Do you really think we could find females here?" Giles sounded so hopeful it annoyed Emit.

"Yeah. Sure. I'd say our chances are really good. Probably as good as living longer than a week with your head bit off,"

Emit said. He looked at his friend whose eyes looked like black pools of despair, and he felt bad for his callous, cynical comment.

"None of the girls back under the sink would even talk to me. I just thought...." Giles ended mumbling into his carapace. He stopped raising his antennae in the air. He pushed up, straightening his front legs and waived his antennae wildly to their left. He ran in circles one way, stopped, and turned to go the opposite.

Emit crossed his eyes and let out a disparaging hiss.

When Giles stopped his confusing antics, he faced to the left, ninety degrees from the direction they had been traveling, and asked, "Would you think I was stupid, or crazy, if...."

"If what?" Emit interrupted. "I already think you're crazy. Stupid is still open for debate, though."

Giles shrugged his right side and pointed his antennae forward. "I get the funniest feeling there's another magic portal this way."

"So, you're magic yourself, now?"

"You don't have to say it like that," Giles said.

To Emit, the words sounded flat, as if Giles weren't listening to his own words. "I guess that direction is as good as any."

Still appearing to be in his own world, Giles crept forward, his antennae flashing up and down, side to side in the purple-red light of setting sun. Emit cleaned his antennae, shrugged his shoulders and followed.

The moon had risen and Emit lost interest in Giles' antics. As they walked, he watched the moon, trying to find in its mottled face the image of the Cockroach Mother and her egg sac. He found, instead, that he had crawled onto his friend's back and arm wrestled Giles' antennae.

"It's over there, in one of those houses."

Giles didn't need to point. It was obvious, now that Emit was paying attention to his surroundings. They had reached the end of ground flattened by the steamrollers. Down a slope of loose rocks, dried weeds, and dirt, was a paved road, across which were several houses.

Emit felt a chill run up his back and looked at his old friend with new respect.

"Which house?" Emit whispered.

"I don't know. It could be any, or all."

Though nothing moved on the ground or in the night sky, they carefully picked their way down the slope, dashed across the road, and crept up the walk to the closest house. They slipped under the door and looked around, testing the air with their antennae.

"There's a portal in here. I feel it, strong," Giles said.

Waving his antennae for confirmation, Emit said, "That may be. I don't feel anything; not food, humans, or roaches."

"Great. We don't want any of that. All we need is a magic portal and cockroach paradise on the other side," Giles said and struck out across the entry room.

They found it before they reached the sink. The portal was in an abandoned mouse hole in a corner of the kitchen. It glowed with hot kaleidoscope colors. Red, orange, and yellow spun and danced beyond the small archway.

"All right. Before we...." Emit had begun to say, but it was too late. Giles leaped through.

"Yes, Giles. I think you're crazy, and yes, I think you're stupid," Emit said to the portal, assuming his friend wouldn't actually hear his words. He crept as close to the portal as he could get, dug his claws into the rotting wooden floor, and without moving the rest of his body, poked his head through the portal.

"Aaaaaaaaaaaaaaaaaah," Giles cried as he slid away from the portal, unable to sink his claws into the surface of this new world. As far as Emit could see there was only glass, as if this portal sat atop a giant opaque globe. The two of them had climbed windows back in their house, but there had been a grimy film, built up from months of neglect, to hold onto. Here, the surface was so clean it appeared wet. Perhaps it was. The momentum of Giles' passage through the portal sent him sliding inexorably away.

"Hey, Giles," Emit called, trying his best not to laugh at his friend's discomfort. "I'm holding the portal open for you. Just fly back."

Giles struggled for a moment longer, then he cocked his head, looking back at Emit. He spread his wings and fluttered into the air, gaining speed until he flashed through the portal and back into the deserted house. A moment later he climbed onto Emit's back and poked his head through the portal, joining his friend to survey the world of glass.

"What is this place?" Giles asked.

"Maybe this is your cockroach paradise," Emit said. "It's just under all this glass."

From their cockroach vantage they were unable to see patterns in the glass delineating the society which had once lived there.

"Not much of a paradise, if you asked me," Giles said and withdrew from the portal.

Emit followed.

Squeezing beneath the front door, they crawled to the edge of the warped wooden porch.

"Maybe one of these other houses has a portal as well," Emit said, cleaning his antennae and waiving them forward.

"There are portals all around us," Giles said. "I can feel them."

"Good," Emit said, eyeing his friend and waving an antenna his direction. He crawled down the side of the porch and onto the grass. "Let's go find a real paradise."

Approaching the next house over, Emit chirped, "I think our luck has just turned for the better, buddy boy. Do you smell that?"

"Yes, sir," Giles said with a smile. "The sweet, musty smell of leaky water pipes."

Antennae waving in anticipation, the friends ran the last ten feet up a gravel path to the house and squeezed beneath the door.

"The kitchen is that way. I can almost taste it," Giles said, about to skitter across the floor.

"Wait. Stop," Emit said, unconsciously cleaning his antennae free of wax, and waved them into the room.

"What's wrong with this picture?"

"What's wrong with it is that we're sitting here on the door step and not under the sink where there's definitely water and probably food as well."

"Yeah. I can smell water, and I can smell food, but what don't you smell?" Emit asked.

"Ummm. Nothing?"

Emit rolled his eyes and fluttered his wings.

"Other cockroaches?"

"Nope. I don't smell any of them," Giles said.

"That's what I mean, Water Bug. If there are leaking pipes under that sink in there, and there is food all around, where are the other cockroaches?"

"Do you want to leave? Try some other place?"

"No. I just don't want to go running into a trap of some kind. Let's take it slow and careful. You follow me, but stay off my tail so I can get a feel for the area."

They skittered slowly along the base of the wall, checking each corner, crack, and crevice for poisons and predators, but found none. They reached the doorway to the kitchen without incident. The drainpipes beneath the sink smelled close now and Emit began to feel as if he had just been paranoid.

"Come on. Let's cross the floor. The sink is right there," Emit said.

"Don't you think it would be safer to follow the baseboards around the room to the sink, like we've been doing?"

"It's right there, five feet away. There could be a cat or possum hiding around a corner. At this point it'd be better to just make a dash for it." Emit could feel the wrongness of his words and the potential for disaster as he spoke them. Before he could voice his change of mind, Giles ran for the cabinet door beneath the kitchen sink.

"Me and my big mouth," Emit said and scurried after his companion.

The two roaches arrived at the base of the cabinet together and Emit ran his antennae through his mandibles and maxillae in relief.

"Wait," Emit screamed and grabbed his friend by the hind set of legs just before they disappeared beneath the cabinet door.

"What now?" Giles whined when he backed out.

"I know what's wrong now. Spiders. Huntsman spiders. Can't you smell them?"

Giles wrinkled his nose, waved his antennae and shrugged two of his three sets of shoulders. "Not really."

"Okay. Look. Let's squeeze under the door, but not all the way into the open. We should just look around before we commit ourselves."

"After you," Giles said with a wave of a clawed hand.

The friends lay side by side, their antennae and heads poking from beneath the door. The smell of water was strong and it dripped constantly from the bend of pipe below the sink. But, just as strong was the smell of the Huntsmen.

"You smell them now?" Emit asked

"Yeah. Like the smell of death, but where are they? Shouldn't there be spider webs?"

"No. The Huntsman spider doesn't weave...."

"Emit," Giles interrupted. "Do you see that?"

"Where?" Emit gasped, pulling back beneath the door.

"No, silly. Look over there. In the corner, just like back home."

Giles was right. In the same corner it had been below the sink in the home where they'd grown up, was a dusty roach motel, and rainbow-mottled lights of a magic portal shimmered from within.

"Let's go," Giles said and launched forward.

"Wait, stupid." Emit grabbed his friend by a back leg.

He pulled him back beneath the door in the nick of time. As he returned to safety, a spider landed with a splat where Giles had been. The creature couldn't reach them beneath the thick wooden door, though they could see the monster clearly. Its two front pairs of legs were obviously longer than those in the rear and the span of its legs could easily cover Emit, his friend and three or four others from the nest back home.

"It, it, it, it," Giles stuttered.

"Yeah. I know. It almost had you. You really need to think before you go scurrying around. In no time, all that will be left of you is wings and legs."

The spider paced back and forth, occasionally nipping at an exposed toe with its mandibles. It stepped back from the door and chittered. Soft clicking sounded from above in response.

"I don't understand spider talk, but I'm willing to bet this guy said there are two juicy cockroaches down here just waiting to be eaten," Emit said.

"I didn't think spiders could talk," Giles said.

"Normally, I'd say you were right. But normally, running through a roach motel only gets you killed and doesn't send you to a strange alternate reality first."

Chittering sounded from outside the cabinet in the kitchen, followed by a plopping sound behind them.

Emit glanced back out from under the door. "Our time just ran out. They have us surrounded and we need to hurry or we'll be dead. You run to that end of the door, I'll take this side. When you hit the wall, don't hesitate, turn and head for the motel. If you make it through the portal and I don't, well, you're on your own. Now, go."

Emit took off like a shot.

"Shouldn't we check to make sure it's safe before we go through?"

Emit wasted precious seconds stopping to turn and tell his friend, "It can't be any more dangerous than sitting here and asking stupid questions. Don't stop when you get there. Run on through."

Giles must have caught on and raced for the wall. Emit didn't watch his friend. They'd have to compare notes if they met up on the other side of this portal. He reached his wall and shot out diagonally across the floor beneath the sink.

The spider was nowhere in sight; it must have gone after Giles. But before he'd gotten ten inches, two more of the creatures dropped down before him. Emit was ready for them as they touched down. He danced quickly to the side. They both pounced toward him. He zigzagged between, hauling cerci toward the roach motel.

The back end of a Huntsman spider stuck out of the near end of the motel, three sets of its legs hugging the exterior of the cardboard box. Emit didn't stop and shot beneath the monster, brushing its belly with his antennae. It slammed its mouth down hard against his exoskeleton, knocking the wind from him, but Emit's momentum carried him through the portal.

The portal popped and disappeared behind him. Giles lay on his back in the middle of a jungle path of wet loam, his knees in the air, three pairs of feet folded together at the center of his abdomen.

Emit crept forward. He tapped his friend with his antennae. "Giles. Buddy. What happened? Those spiders weren't poisonous."

Giles opened an eye and whispered, "I know. I'm playing dead. I think there are monkeys in the trees."

Emit turned his eyes and surveyed the jungle around him. The lush foliage around him was wet from the heavy, humid, air, but could see no monkeys. Not wanting an argument, he said, "Monkeys don't care if you're dead or alive. They'll eat you either way. Let's get off this trail."

Emit scrambled through the wet grass to hide beneath a large leaf, expecting Giles to follow. Once safely beneath a philodendron, he turned and looked back. Giles hadn't moved.

"Are you crazy? Get out of the open. It's not safe out there," Emit screamed at his friend.

Giles' voice was faint, almost indiscernible from the continuous rattle of water dripping from trees above the jungle trail. "What's the use? If the monkeys don't get us, the rats or the centipedes will. Just go on without me."

Emit saw the monkeys then, and understood his friend's despair.

Monkeys huddled together on branches; they clutched the trunks of trees and sheltered beneath large, elephant-ear-shaped leaves. Emit felt that each monkey, with its surprised little monkey eyes in its furry little monkey head, was staring at him and only him, biding its little monkey time, just waiting for the right moment to dash forward and snatch him from his hiding place.

The path wound out of the distant, dark, jungle foliage, curved past Emit's hiding place and off to other places just as dark and just as dangerous as whence it came. Legs in the air, Giles lay just a few feet away.

Emit suddenly felt lost and helpless. Giles was his friend and had been since they were newly out of their mothers' egg sacs. Though his friend was daring and impetuous, he had endless optimism and enthusiasm. Now, he was broken and giving up.

Sure. It was Giles' fault they were here, awaiting death at the greedy hands and teeth of monkeys, but the dilemma was now Emit's; he could only escape the jungle with Giles' help.

"Giles," Emit whispered.

Giles didn't move.

"Giles, buddy. Listen to me," Emit rasped in as low a voice a middle-aged cockroach could manage. Still no response.

Emit crept to the edge of his concealing leaf. With each step closer to his supine friend, the tension between him and the monkeys seemed build until one more step would make it explode. "Giles. I need you."

Giles turned his head to Emit, and raised a single antenna. "You don't need me. I'm the one who brought us here, and nearly got us squashed by rolling machines, and also nearly got us eaten by spiders. For what? A cockroach paradise? No. For a jungle death trap where we can do nothing but wait to be eaten by monkeys, or rats, or birds, or possums, or frogs or who knows what else. Do you see any houses? No. Of course not. We're in a jungle."

"No, dude. You can get us out of here. Only you. I can't feel the magic like you can. Try it, buddy. Feel for a portal like you did before. See if you can feel one that will take us back home. Tell me which way to go so we can high tail it out of here. Point us to another portal."

Giles looked up. "You believe me, now? That I can feel the magic?"

"I do, brother, I really do. And I need you to do it. Because if you don't say which way to run soon, it's not going to matter. These monkeys are starting to move."

Giles smiled, surprise gleaming in his dark eyes.

Emit leaned forward. "Can you feel it? Can you feel the portal?"

"I can," Giles said, rolling over. "Come on."

Giles shot back up the trail in the direction they had just come, Emit close on his tail.

With a mad pandemonium of screams and hoots, the monkeys broke from their stasis and raced after the two roaches.

Emit and Giles dodged hanging vines and gnarled roots, racing over the damp earth. With each step, the howling pack of primates got closer.

"Fly," Emit cried and the two took to the air, out of reach of clawing monkey fingers.

Birds darted down to take up the chase from where the monkeys dropped off, and the roaches swirled, dived, and barrel rolled around creepers and trees, returning to the path and racing along the jungle floor. They shot beneath dripping plants and through moldering leaves.

"There it is," Giles said, sounding as surprised as Emit felt. In the distance, shining like a beacon through the crepuscular half-light of heavy jungle was a tiny circular glow.

Emit saw it but knew it was too far away. Monkeys hooted and laughed as they converged on the narrow path. Birds of all sizes and colors shot back and forth across their way, their calls both sinister and taunting. Like a nightmare, the soft earth beneath their scampering feet boiled and burst open, releasing every vicious creature Emit had ever seen or heard tell of: centipedes, scorpions and great hairy spiders, skunks, opossums, and rats, many out of place in an Eden of primeval jungle. All gathered around the small box that promised their only escape.

Running and flying, dodging and ricocheting off one another, Giles and Emit evaded grasping fingers, sharp beaks, and poison stingers. Poised and ready to pounce, predators of all kinds gathered around the portal leading from the jungle-world.

Emit shot past his friend as they passed the deadly gauntlet around the gleaming exit.

He thought it was oddly surreal, like a frozen scene from a dream where everything spins around you, yet nothing actually moves. Claws extended, teeth gleaming, mandibles spread wide, the animals were a horror of statuary; a deadly, immobile tableau. Expecting his head to be ripped from his body, he tucked his antennae behind him and closed his eyes as he leaped for the magic portal.

A familiar tingle washed across his exoskeleton as he passed through swirling colors. Hitting the ground of this new world, Emit flattened himself and waited to be eaten.

Something was different. He waved his antennae to get a sense of the place.

"Emit. Open your eyes," Giles whispered from nearby. "Hey, Emit. Are you awake?"

There was his answer: he'd been dreaming. And now he could open his eyes and find himself back in his old nest in the safety of the cabinet beneath the kitchen sink. He opened the eye closest to the sound of his friend and quickly looked around. He jumped to all six feet.

"You got us home. Dude," Emit said and glanced over his back at the roach motel in the corner. The portal remained open, shimmering back at him like a winking eye. "Let's get back to the nest where it's safe and I can give my poor heart a rest."

Emit skittered toward an open seam between boards at the back corner of the cabinet until he realized Giles wasn't following him. His friend crouched near the open end of the roach motel staring into the shifting, mottled colors and absently cleaning his antennae.

"Dude. Come on. Let's get back into the nest. We can chat up some of the newly molted females."

"I was just thinking, would this portal take us back to the rolling machines, or do you think it would take us someplace different? You know," Giles said, scratching an eye. "Now that I know how to use the magic, we could explore all we want. I could always bring us back home whenever we need."

"Give it up, dude. There's no magic. It was dumb luck we ended up back at home."

"But you said...."

Emit cut him off. "I said what I had to, to get you moving again. You'd have died there on that trail, otherwise. It was just coincidence we found a portal back to our nest. Now, come on. Let's go home and relax."

For the second time, Emit realized his friend wasn't following. He stopped and called to Giles, "Oh for pity's sake, guy. Be a cockroach and let's go nest."

When there was no reply, Emit turned back around to find his friend was no longer in the cabinet beneath the sink.

Inferno Land

by Charlie Brown

Canto I

In the middle of my journey, I found the place deep within those woods on the Florentine edges where my hero departed this world for someplace stranger and forbidden.

The red fir trees along the mule paths grew without design, but on the fourth day of my excursions within these hills, I saw a group forming a perfect circle that fit the description I'd found while in the city. I stood within the ring, the world outside hushed and still, and felt dizzy, my vision blurring and a vortex forming above my head. I should have run, but instead embraced the mystery because this was where I wanted – no, needed – to be.

But I should tell you why I traveled so far from home in the first place. I was approaching the end of my doctoral program in literature at Chapman University, just south of Los Angeles in Orange County. While my professors admitted my work was sound and my scholarship impeccable, they couldn't hide their disappointment that someone named Peter Gonzales, a café-con-leche-skinned and raven-haired Mexican, had no interest in Latin American literature. Why wouldn't I dive into Garcia Marquez, Borges, or at the very least Allende? Wouldn't a young Hispanic in a post-millennial society have great insight into technology versus magical realism? Or something of the sort. Didn't I want to get published? And tenure?

But my heart lived in the Renaissance and its poetic epics. I kept that famous portrait of Dante Alighieri above my writing desk; his eyes locked down into a squint, his shirt collar squared like a parish priest's, and the formidable hat, banded across the scalp and gathered into a stocking-like end flowing past his shoulders like a maiden's tresses. And I have read *The Divine Comedy* many times through, first in translation, then in the original as I began my dissertation.

How do you describe a first love? In 1996, my Beatrice was a sixth-grade teacher at John Muir Middle School on Vermont Street in the heart of South Central L.A. The neighborhood contained dingy stores, signs in Spanish, and cruddy streets filthy as the Angelino air. But Ms. D'agostino, a dwarfish and pale woman who favored cotton floral prints with Birkenstock sandals and quoted Nirvana and Pearl Jam daily, saw me trolling the sorry stacks of the school library searching for something similar to *Lord of the Rings*.

"It may take you a while to get this," she said, pulling a book from the poetry section and fiddling with her thick, black-framed glasses. "But it will help you understand so many things when you do."

I, flushed with blooming puberty, felt my first female attraction that day, but reading those skimpy lines and short cantos put me on my true life path.

But when I was close to finishing my dissertation, a close examination of the political realities between Guelfs and Ghibellines that defined so many of the characters within the epic, I found my text lacking, the level of verisimilitude not deep enough for my exacting standards. I needed to leave southern California and put myself into Dante's world.

After five months of applications and justifications, I obtained a grant to spend three weeks in Florence. Once there, I worked harder than I ever had before, looking into every relevant record and archive to find those details which would take my prose from pedestrian to divine.

Turns out Dante scholarship is a cottage industry in that walled city. Like the mule paths cutting into the Alpine trails, I trod well-worn ground. But there was a string running through all the records, a "lost" confession made by the poet after he had disappeared for two weeks.

Only after an evening's reflection aided by Chianti did it occur to me: could the poem be real? Was it transcription, not invention? After many inquiries among Thoth-like archivists, most avoiding the subject or downright denying it, I found a sympathetic soul.

Viggo Maccinato, a rotund Italian whose chalk-white hair formed a natural tonsure, overheard my pleas in the Medici Archives and pulled me aside, telling his colleague he would explain to the stupid American in as simple English as he could muster that what I wanted existed in the realm of the impossible. But while his words contained admonishment, he handed me a card with an address and time written on the back.

The blocky apartment house stood in the shadow of City Hall's spire, but while it looked old, it didn't look like a repository. Maccinato arrived fifteen minutes late, but he brought a glass of wine for me from his dinner engagement.

"But drink it quickly," he said in Italian. "It will not be allowed inside."

After we imbibed, he rang the bell and the door buzzed. We pushed through the door, its locking mechanism state of the art. Inside was only an ascending staircase, which led to a steel door that opened with an audible *whoosh*. The climate-controlled room within was sterile white, the back wall lined with crumbling manuscripts held behind glass.

Maccinato introduced Mr. Ferriday, a square-headed Englishman in a doctor's coat who stood a full foot taller than me. "This one 'ere. 'Ees all right then?" His accent was pugnacious Cockney.

"I have-a tracked his-a moving around-a da city," Maccinato answered in halting English. "He a-seem-a to be dedicato."

"Dat right?" The man glared at me, his nose and chin squinching closer with menace. I quoted from memory the first twenty lines of "Inferno." He nodded, but didn't soften. "I'll get the confession." He keyed numbers into a pad and pulled the vault open. He lifted a glass case, setting it on a rubber-topped desk, then loomed over me, jabbing his gloved finger just shy of my breastbone. "No touching!"

I sat and read. When I reached for my notebook, Maccinato tapped my shoulder and tsked. I read as quickly as I could. Dante had been lost among the goat trails, but he found a perfect circle of firs. After that, he awoke in Florence having lost time. Afterward, he wrote his masterpiece.

I stood, my task finished. Ferriday pointed me to a book by the front door. "Please sign out."

I grabbed the pen on the end of a chain and stood before the ledger. The last inscription was from 1989. "Is this true?" My voice squealed with shock.

"Right-o, mate. You're my number two. Job's lonely, but it pays well."

Maccinato said he was going to keep his friend company for a while, so I ran outside. After scribbling down everything I could remember, I went in search of hiking boots.

And so I stood ready to feel the pull of the vortex, hoping and praying I would return to this world because my curiosity was too strong and my love for Dante too deep to let this opportunity disappear.

Canto II

After a brief blackness, I still stood within the firs. I felt I couldn't trust my vision, as the air blurred and bent light into glowing shafts, like sunshine reflecting off a watch face. I rubbed my eyes, but heard a rumbling growl coming from a few feet away.

Looking around, I saw I was surrounded. While I trembled from danger, I was also thrilled at what appeared before me: a leopard, a lion, and a she-wolf, the three beasts who drove Dante to the gates of Hell.

They entered the circle and spoke to me in unaccented English. "Leave this place. Leave this place," they threatened, but I wasn't sure how I could follow their directions. They had left my back open, so I turned and ran, hoping to appease their anger.

I had another moment of blackout, then arrived at an infinite gray plain. The despair I felt looking upon the vastness overwhelmed me and I fell to my knees. After a few more moments where I struggled to keep tears within their ducts, the vortex that brought me here opened again, expulsing the menacing animals. I braced for a mauling, but instead their mood turned welcoming, nudging me around until I saw a closed gate, twenty feet tall and black as a seasoned cast-iron pan. Above it were letters forming the phrase I knew so well: "Abandon hope all ye who enter here."

I stood, awed by the infinite unknown I faced. Behind that enclosure were the sinful; those who spent their time on Earth fulfilling only their desires with no regard for others. This place was why I still went to Sunday Mass, confessed my sins, and had retained my virginity until I found the woman I would marry. I looked to the beasts to find the way forward.

They popped up on their back legs and danced, their front paws flowing and waving like jazz hands (jazz paws?) until they sang a burlesque of a Broadway song bolstered by an unseen band:

"Abandon hope all ye who enter here,
"The righteous tremble and the sinful fear,
"Even though you wonder how the evil play,
"Run through the gates and enjoy your daaaaaay!"

They formed a kickline and bounced through their big finish.

"Abandon hope all ye who enter here,
"But now you know that fun is near,
"And now the man who will show you the way,
"The epic poet, Daaaaaa-ah-aaaan-taaaaaaay!"

The gates opened and a man exited in a smoky flash. As he approached, I recognized the Roman nose of my hero who, when he stood in front of me, came up just under my nipples.

I had no idea he was so short.

After introductions, he put his arm around my waist and led me to the open doors. "Come, Pietro, we must not-a delay." His English was very similar to Maccinato's. "But I-uh have to let-a you know. They have made-a some changes since-a my book."

We passed through the gates of Hell, I relieved to be away from that dreadful desert. We were transported to an enormous cave, milky stalactites the size of the moon rockets drooping from a ceiling so high I couldn't see the top from the lack of light. Right in front of a sludgy river hung a sign on two poles ending in wicked spear tips: "Welcome to Inferno Land!"

"But don't worry," my guide said. "They made-a it more fun!"

Canto III

Dante led me under the sign to a dock where a dilapidated gondola rocked in the slow current. The boatman, cloaked in heavy black canvas, stood next to his oar, the end crusted with barnacles.

"Charon?" I wondered how closely this "new" Hell might cleave to the cantos.

"Si, si. He like-a to take all across a-personally."

The two of us climbed in, sitting on the unpadded crossbar. Dante faced forward, but I turned to see the legendary gondolier. His body was completely skeletal, no hair or skin remaining on the few revealed parts. I think he was trying to smile at me, but he had no uplifting tendons to make it look welcoming. I nodded and returned his smile while trying not to look nervous, but had to turn around to gaze in the same direction as my companion so as not to contemplate Charon's eerie visage.

As we floated away from the dock, I asked, "What happened here?"

"Oh, you know." Dante looked casual, although I could sense a deeper regret. "A time ago, it's-a hard to tell exactly down here, maybe one-a hundred of Earth's years, we stopped getting the big-a crowds. I think-a maybe the boss' contract with Cielo, what you call it? Heaven? That-a lapsed. Now, we-a try to get-a some new customers."

"But how could someone as pious as you end up in Inferno?"

"Oh!" A chuckle escaped with the exclamation. "No! I choose-a to come here. Lucifer, he say-a my poem is-a da good PR."

As we reached the halfway point of the river Acheron, I heard a sound like an ancient door opening. Our navigator had started singing "O sole mio" in a dusty voice that made Tom Waits sound like Maria Callas. The tune scraped my soul like a garden rake through loamy topsoil.

Dante rocked with the singing. "We-a trying to attract-a the Venice crowd, eh?" He put his hand to the side of his mouth, whispering, "He-a expecting the tip."

I dug in my pocket for Euro coins, dropping them in a basket next to the boatman's bony feet. Charon sang even louder, but I would have given the entirety of my bank account to have that lipless mouth quit.

Finally, we reached the far bank. After bowing to Charon, Dante led me to a glass-enclosed structure. "This is-a Limbo. We have-a remade for the vino, yes?"

"Limbo is a wine bar?"

"The best in Inferno!"

Canto IV

Dante pulled open the door, the glass leaded and held together by brass. Inside were many curly-haired men and women clad in togas and drinking from silver wineglasses. They all looked like the classical marble statues in the J. Paul Getty Museum come to life.

A blond man picked a lute in the corner, a haunting tune casting a melancholy mood over the crowd. Dante clapped his hands in admonishment.

"Hey, Orpheo, this is-a no funeral. Pep it-a up!" The man plucked faster at his instrument, making the air lighter and cups tip faster. "There you a-go. Bene, bene. Pietro, you must-a come to-a da corner of poets."

He scooted to the back corner away from the door, stopping at a table with two gentlemen; Roman-looking from the construction of the togas. The one to my left, slight and pale, propped his head up with his hand, looking as if being awake were torture. The other, Falstaffian in waistline and beard, scanned the room and ignored Dante as he introduced us.

"Meet Virgil and Horace, my friends and boon companions." Virgil waved at me with limp wrists while Horace gave me as much attention as he had Dante. "We have-a had da many nights, talking and telling stories. Being here with-a my heroes has been so enlightening, yes?"

Dante sat next to Virgil who said, "I'm not giving the tour this time, am I?"

"No, this-a one is-a mine."

"Great! Take a seat kid."

Horace's face reddened as he looked to the bar. "For Jupiter's sake, we ordered the wine flight. How can I carpe diem if I can't carpe vino?" Finally, he looked me in the face and said, "What fresh Hell are you?"

"Watch your mouth!" Virgil lifted his head, peeved at his friend. "This good chap is a paying customer."

Horace's anger turned into an unctuous smile. "Well, I'll be damned. Too late, right?" His elbow found its way into my ribs, a jab hard enough that I had to rub the spot. "Now you, good sir, could get us some of the good stuff. Boy!"

A blond, teenaged-looking youngster in a very short tunic arrived tableside. Dante looked at a list written on papyrus. "Our-a guest wants only da finest. You bring-a for all, yes?"

"Yes," I said, glad to be able to spend time with such famous poets.

"That Gitone is such a good-looking lad." Horace shook a head full of rue, then popped another elbow into my sore side. "Gets more ass than a mule farmer, if you know what I mean."

The flight of short wine glasses, each holding only a few sips, came within a minute. Dante and Virgil talked about park business while Horace pointed out all the women he wanted to sleep with. None were yet forthcoming.

I took a sip from the first glass. While my companions lit up, their palates enthralled, my mouth puckered in shock, the liquid so sweet it tasted like a wine Slurpee. Each offering was worse than the other, my tongue revolting from the worst wine I've ever had. And I've drunk Manischewitz.

Virgil leaned across the table. "Kid, when you've been in Limbo for as long as we have, your senses get dull. We need the extra jolt just to feel anything." He finished the last of his flight, bobbing with pleasure. "Oh, that's so good."

"We can-a tarry no longer, Pietro. Is-a time for the Grand Tour!" Dante jumped up, patted the poets on the back and ran out the front door. I turned to Horace.

"Don't let us keep you, buddy. There are much better things to see."

As I left the wine bar, Dante waved me over to a booth where a Greek-looking man with a twined gray mustache waited inside.

"Meet Minos." The former king of Knossos had no chair, sitting on his serpentine tail coiled like a spring. "He's-a in charge of-a da tickets."

Dante wandered away to let us transact, but I was confused. "I don't have much money."

Minos waved his hand. "We don't deal with the lucre, per se. Anyone passing through Inferno Land gives his soul a short respite before disappearing to Heaven."

"How much is the tour?"

"Our basic passage means you spend one day in Purgatory. With that, Dante gives you the tour, the rides that go with them and lunch at the food court."

"That sounds okay to me."

"Wait a sec. That's the basic. For a few days in Inferno, we can offer some premium packages."

"I, uh..."

"Listen, these get you all the sin you can handle. Extra greedy, extra wrathful..." He wiggled his eyebrows at me and exaggerated his voice. "Extra lusty. Don't you wanna?"

"No," I said, worms wriggling through my belly. "The basic is good enough."

"Whatever." He ripped a red fair ticket from the end of a spool and handed it to me.

"Come on-a, now. We have-a to catch-a da ride." Dante tugged at my wrist.

As I followed, something flashed through my mind. "Wait," I called to Minos. "How long is a day in Purgatory?"

"Have a good time," he said, waving and rolling down the booth's shutter.

Canto V

Dante led me to a ride line, its twisty path set off by crumbling plastic chains and rusty silver poles. As there was no one else queuing, we went straight to the front.

"Today, you-a getting the express-a pass."

A wooden sign with a scarlet devil looking like the one on the canned ham package held up a pitchfork. It read, "You must be this tall to ride." I was a full two feet above the upper prick of his trident.

Behind the gate was a circular cement spot with a platform in the middle bearing a seat looking like a ski lift. There were no wires leading up, but Dante and I sat. He pulled down the bar and told to me hold tight.

"But wh..." I couldn't finish my question before a shadow streaked across the sky and we were airborne. Gripping the sides for fear of falling, I looked up to see the top of our ride was pulled by two talons, which were connected to huge bat wings and a long snaky tale. "G-G-Geryon?" I yelled, as the wind in my face cut most noise to my ears.

"Si!" Dante looked exuberant as we flew between the layers of Hell, each granite-like circle looking like stacked storm clouds. "Look-a! No hands!" He held up his arms, hat trailing behind like a windsock.

First, we flew through the forest of living trees. Geryon swung our carriage right and left to avoid the whipping ends of their branches. But not all were enthusiastic, as I saw one oak look away from us and swing like an old man dismissing a child.

We next descended into the Tomb of Heresies (as the giant sign indicated), a rounded cave like a train tunnel that could fit the Titanic. Up and down Geryon flew over, shooting flames like a steeplechase. At the exit, Geryon flew too low and the bottoms of my hiking boots were singed.

As we shot out, the dragon zoomed upward, heading for a grassy ledge.

"Cover your mouth. Here come-a the Styx." Dante screamed and clasped both hands over his jaw line. I did the same.

The knoll was the levee for the River of Forgetfulness, where a muddy patch led to the running waters. Geryon dipped us deep in the muck while ghastly warriors poked at us with spears and swords.

"Feel our wrath," they chanted, but none gained purchase with their weapons.

Rising back into the air, I saw my clothes caked in filth and hoped to get clean soon. I didn't know my wish would be granted so quickly.

We splashed into the Styx, immediately drenched in the waves of the wide river. I knew any sip would erase my memory, but that was least among my problems. Premiere on that list was my stomach, quavering after all that shaking.

Geryon set us down on a new landing and I rolled out as soon as Dante lifted the bar. On my hands and knees, I vomited. Unfortunately, my expectum washed over sandaled feet.

I looked up to see a Greek man, beard trim and hair wavy, quite handsome, if hangdog. Across his right arm was a pile of T-shirts, his extended left holding out a single one. "Most everyone wants one of these after the rides."

"How much will it cost?"

"A mere ten minutes in Purgatory."

Even though the air was warm, I still felt chilled by the waters and exchanged my shirt for one of his. I held it up before slipping it over my head. Pictured was a cartoon Geryon, tongue lolling and eyes bugging, while overly animated riders screamed. It reminded me of the worst shirts at Knott's Berry Farm. However ugly it was, dryness was the real issue. The man held my waterlogged polo.

"First time here?" He looked bored.

"Yes. I imagine you get many like me."

"Not as much as you'd think. I'm Ulysses, by the way."

"The Ulysses? Of Ithaca?"

"One and the same, my good man. I see my renown remains down there."

"Boys all over the world read of your journey home from Troy."

"Damn. You get lost once and nobody lets you forget it."

"How did you escape from the flames?" Dante's description of the master trickster engulfed in fire in the eighth circle was the image that haunted me the most in the epic.

"Satan let me off the hook when the park opened. Figured I'd be right for design and retail."

"This place is your idea?"

"Parts of it. You bought a T-shirt, didn't you?" An oily smile crawled across his mouth as he saluted me and walked off whistling.

Canto VI

My torso dry in the new garb, I ran my hands through my hair to wick away the remaining river droplets. I didn't want any bit to find its way to my tongue because I didn't want to forget these experiences.

Dante pointed over a hill. "Pietro, is-a time for lunch, no?"

I admitted I was ravenous and we climbed the easy incline. Just over the ridge was a city clouded in sticky shadows. "Is that Dys?"

Dante nodded, leading me down the path.

I remembered the lines from the poem, how one of Heaven's angels appeared to get Dante past the demon guards. We arrived at the wrought iron gates, evil-weaved bars ending in sharp horns, but they were open. Tied along the top were strings ending in balloons, probably once inflated with helium, but now hanging withered like raisined grapes. A white vinyl sign, grimy with coppery dirt, was slung over the opening.

Dys, the horrible city of demons, was now the food court.

"Where are the demons? Do they not stand guard anymore?"

"They found-a the new-a job." Walking through the gate, we saw three scaly creatures, wings tucked into their backs, surrounding a cardboard rectangle and old-school boom box while popping and locking to a hip-hop beat. I recognized the song as Herbie Hancock's "Rockit."

"Yo, yo, Dante dawg. Check this shit out." The demon sounded like a choking frog, which made my stomach turn. He dropped straight into his break-dancing routine, spinning on his back, then rolling into an inch worm. But as he started whirling on his head, one of his horns caught the cardboard, collapsing the whole routine in a mess of snaky tail and clawed foot.

"You-a so much better! You-a, how they say, funky fresh."

The demon held up the tip jar, his smile full of pointy razors. I was running low on cash, but dared not refuse to drop some in the bucket. I remembered that lunch was included with my package, so Dante led me to a three-stooled diner that looked like an old-fashioned hot dog stand.

As we sat, a harpy flew over, order pad in her claws, hair constructed into a ziggurat-y beehive and a cigarette dangling from her lips. We picked up the menus and I asked what the house special was.

"The liver is the best, doll." Somehow her bird-like cluck had a Brooklyn accent.

"I haven't had liver in years. That sounds good."

But then I heard a male voice scream, "By all the gods, no! Don't get the liver!" I jumped out of my seat and ran to the back of the diner where a naked man was chained to a rock.

"Prometheus?" I took his pained gargle as assent. Just above his bare buttocks was an open wound, his purple liver pulsing, waiting to be cut out and regenerated.

He wailed again and I saw another harpy wearing the

squat white toque of the short-order cook in a tree above him, a gleaming butcher's knife dangling in her left claw. "We also like it when people order the tongue."

Too squeamish to eat, I rejoined my companion and took another look at the menu. I told the waitress harpy I wanted a milkshake.

"Sure thing, babe. Be right back."

Dante nodded at my choice. "The milkshakes are-a surprisingly a-good."

As he looked to see what he might order, I heard a loud snort and a bovine yawp. I turned to see a minotaur dash by, bottom half female and nude, her deflated breasts flopping and squishing as she ran. The waitress flew after her, breast pump in her claw.

"I don't think I'm thirsty anymore."

Dante looked at a watch. "Then we must hurry! The grand finale awaits!"

Canto VII

Finally, we trekked across the icy plains of the ninth circle. Dante pulled at my wrist like a three-year-old dragging his mother away from the dress shop and toward the candy counter.

"Pietro, we must hurry. The show is about to start and it will not happen again for another hour."

I knew exactly what awaited us at the end of the path. Had I not pored over my guide's text? Who could forget the horrific vision he described to keep the righteous on the good path?

The way wound around blindingly white mounds, hills so far beneath the wintry surface they looked like scoops of vanilla ice cream forgotten in the back of the freezer, overcome by crystals and solid beyond consumption. But as we made our way past the tallest of them all, Dante's face exploded with joy.

I saw the curving horns first, the distance between the ground and its tip roughly the same as the height of the Empire State Building. The full visage of Lucifer, three goat heads buried to the neck in the tundra, overwhelmed me and I fell into the frost. His skin maintained a chillingly bluish hue and icicles the size of Amtrak trains drooped from his chin. I felt like a gnat on his own neck; small and insignificant in the face of the Great Satan.

And yet I felt acknowledged, that this horrifying beast had been waiting for me, a speck of dust on his nostril. I looked to Dante who brimmed with excitement, bobbing on toes and heels. He had described what was to happen as a "show," but gazing upon the vast fallen angel gave me no clue what that could mean.

Then a stabbing piano rang out from no discernible sound system. I recognized the panic-inducing pattern immediately. Like the vilest Country Bears at the evilest Chuck E. Cheese known to creation, tri-headed Lucifer sang Foreigner's "Cold As Ice."

Describing the three-part harmonized voice as basso profundo greatly underestimates the sound belching out. Like the electronic bottom vibrating your clothes in a cranked-up club, this voice did the same to my bowels. I was pleased not to soil myself despite the great pain of restraining my inner effluvium.

I looked to see how the poet could stand it, but he stood banging his head, hand raised in heavy metal horns. Maybe it was a protection against the evil eye, like Ronnie James Dio's Sicilian grandmother taught the diminutive singer before his fame. But, in truth, I had to accept that Dante was rocking out.

The song came to the bridge, where the two side heads sang counterpoint echoes of the titular words while the center head interjected, "You know that you are!" The awful evilness overwhelmed me and I turned to my guide for help, greatly desiring escape from this nightmarish karaoke. But he swayed and waved his hands like a hippie girl at Woodstock, oblivious to my suffering.

In this final image of my hero, my brain took off its shoes and ran barefoot away from my consciousness.

Epilogue

I awoke in a Florentine hospital. Informed I was found in the woods and had been in a coma for two weeks, I sank into the bed and felt around my body. I was still whole, but my mind still felt outside my meat suit. The doctor took my pulse and walked out without a further word.

But the nurse lingered, speaking to me in Italian. "You talked in your state. It's very unusual. I didn't know what you were saying, but one of the doctors said you were chanting Dante."

"What about the band Foreigner?"

"You sang that right before you woke up."

They kept me under observation for two more weeks. While the hospital's psychiatrist tried to convince me I had suffered delusions while in the catatonic state, he had no explanation for the T-shirt of the dragon splashing in black waters.

I returned to Los Angeles, but despite an extension of my deadline, I couldn't work up the strength to finish my dissertation. My professors pleaded with me to finish, knowing my ABD status would disqualify me from many jobs, but I couldn't write with scrambled eggs for brains.

After my fifth debilitating panic attack, I checked myself into Promises, a place usually reserved for drug addicts and alcoholics, but also a peaceful respite for those of us hanging onto sanity by our fingernails.

Because it wasn't just the experience I had been through. It was the thought that anywhere I went, be it the mall or the gym or any public place where classic rock would be broadcast, the ice pick voice of Lou Graham would belt out his song and my brain would once again bubble over.

By the good Lord above, I've always hated that song.

Welcome to the Deluxe Dairy

by J.R. Murdock

"Junior! You need to go check Daisy."

"But Pa, you just checked her a couple days ago."

"Yeah, and she might be ready. I don't wanna take no chances. Now get! And don't give me none of your excuses today. My leg's bad and I ain't got time to check her. Just remember, she's a special cow and you need to be careful, ya hear?"

"Yeah, I hear."

Pa had been a cattle farmer all his life, just as I had been. Growing up on the farm, you found things you loved and things you hated to do. Running a dairy farm, Deluxe Dairy in Rochester, Minnesota, I'd learned that cows could be big, stupid, and mean. I'd been chased, kicked, bumped, and even knocked down. I'd done everything on that farm at least once.

Everything except check a heifer's baby.

Pa had always done that and it did not look like anything I wanted to try. I'd come up with all kinds of excuses over the years. He'd slipped on some manure and Daisy had stomped on him the day before yesterday and he'd been real ornery since. It was time to prove I had what it took.

Sure, I knew all about checking the cows. I'd been there with Pa dozens of times as he checked. He usually made me hold the tail up real high while he ran his arm in the backside of a cow. You just needed to feel down once your arm was in up to the shoulder, and you could feel the calf.

"Fine, I'll go check." I wanted to say something else, but I knew that'd earn me a whuppin' from Pa. He didn't like no back talk and I wasn't about to give any.

In the coatroom I put on my work boots and coveralls. Tending to cows was messy work on a good day. When checking a heifer's calf, it was a bad day. The stink of birthing a calf could be with you for days if you weren't careful.

I hopped on the John Deere quad utility vehicle and rode out to the barn where all the pregnant heifers were. Those closest to giving birth were kept separate from the milking herd. Daisy, one of our best heifers, was at the far end of the barn. I took the quad all the way around the barn to her stall.

The shoulder-length latex gloves were hung on the outside of each stall of the pregnant ones. I grabbed one, opened the gate, and went in. Daisy wasn't in a good mood. She knew what was coming and was having none of it.

"Come on girl. I don't like this any more than you do. Let's just get this over with and we can both have a better day after, all right?"

She charged me. I ran back out the gate and closed it. She came up short and thankfully didn't hit the gate. I reached over and locked it, watching her between the slats.

"It's gonna happen, one way or another."

She mooed at me and then, I'm quite sure this was deliberate, sneezed through her nose at me. I closed my eyes and mouth just in time, but slimy snot ran down my face.

There were times I felt bad when Pa donned the glove and checked the cows. I never wanted to do it because the cows sure didn't look like they enjoyed it at all. Now I wanted to make sure Daisy didn't enjoy this one.

"That's the way you want to play it?" I wiped the snot off my face. "Fine. Let's play."

I wasn't able to get inside with her. She was blocking me from getting in, and would run if I pulled the gate open. If I were to get Daisy in the gate for checking, I needed to trick her. Normally me and Pa would do this together and just push, but he'd taught me a trick when doing this alone.

A bushel of apples sat at the door to the barn. I grabbed one, cut it in half, and passed one half through the gate. Daisy ate it up. The girls loved their apples. As she chewed, she allowed me to come back into her pen. I held out the other half and led her over to the gate.

She stopped in front of it.

"Come on, girl. You like apples. These are better than that crummy old hay and grass. Come on."

She started moving again, but slowly. She followed me into the gate and got her head all the way through and I gave her the apple. I had to run around the backside to close her in, but I had her. Finally.

I went back to the gate to pick up the glove I'd dropped. It was dirty, so I had to grab me another and got the OB lube as well. Once I had the glove well greased, I pulled a work glove onto my left hand with my teeth and went to check Daisy's business end.

I didn't want to waste no time so I grabbed her tail and raised it high. Since I'd never done this, I wanted to make sure I was doing everything right. Pa is about a half-foot taller than me, so my shoulder wasn't at the right height. I was going to need the stool.

Once the stool was in place, I was a little higher than Daisy's entry. The glove was lubed and pulled up to the shoulder. This was it. I was going in. I put my hand straight, locked my wrist, and started pushing.

Daisy wasn't happy and pushed back. The lube made it a little easier to push in, but Daisy was strong. Sure, I knew she was big, but I wasn't expecting this.

My arm was only in up to my elbow, but I felt something warm moving.

"No!"

I hopped off the stool, pulled my arm out, and moved to

the side of Daisy just as she sprayed fresh manure all over the pen. I'd have to clean that up before I was done. She'd been pushing so hard it even sprayed the wall.

I shook off what was on the glove. "Daisy, that was nasty."

Hopefully she was empty now. I got back up on my stool, raised her tail, and went in again. Of course she resisted, but with the way mostly clear I was able to keep pushing inside. I was almost done.

Or so I thought.

I got in nearly to my shoulder and started feeling for her cervix. I found that and could feel the baby's head. I ran my hand up a little higher and I could feel the rest of the baby. It was facing the right way and would be a normal birth. Everything was looking good. Based on the movement of the calf, it would probably come in the next couple days.

Something pulled my hand. A contraction? I wondered if my checking her had caused Daisy to go into labor. The pulling stopped, but once I started to pull my hand free, it jerked again. It pulled me up to my shoulder and my face slammed against Daisy's backside.

I dropped the tail and put my hand on her hindquarters and struggled to get free. My arm started coming out, but only a tiny bit. Whatever was pulling me, it was strong. I tried to think if, in all the years of Pa and I checking the cows, anything like this had ever happened. When my face slammed into Daisy's back end again, I stopped trying to think if it'd happened and just tried to figure a way out of this mess.

Daisy mooed and shifted to the side.

"I know! I know! I don't want my arm in you any more either. Just hold still."

Everything had been warm inside of Daisy, but my hand grew cold. It felt like I'd just stuck it into a snowbank. I didn't like this, not one little bit. I had to get my arm free. Pa wouldn't be coming to check on me for some time, and I did not want him to find me like this.

My fingers started to tingle. It felt as if the glove was dissolving away and I felt cold ground under my fingers.

Then something licked me. A thick, rough tongue.

"Oh this ain't happening. Pa! Pa! Come help me!"

It made no difference if he could hear me or not; I was yelling. I needed to get my arm out of Daisy. I pulled as hard as I could, but it wasn't budging.

Then it pulled harder. Some glow came from Daisy's back end and it opened up wider. That's when the rest of me got pulled inside.

At first it was warm, just like when I'd stuck my arm up inside Daisy. Then it was cold like sitting outside on a winter's night. I couldn't see nothing at first. It was all cold and dark. I had the feeling I was sitting in the woods, but it was difficult to make out shapes.

I took the glove off my arm. I didn't need it no more. My phone was still in my pocket so I got it out, turned it on, and shined it around.

Paths led off in several directions. Trees, black and dead, sat on all sides of me. I shined the light, but couldn't see nothing clearly past a few feet.

Something nudged me from behind. I spun around and fell onto my back. I was going to die. I just knew death was near. I'd dropped my phone and I could see the eerie, black branches over me like the fingers of Death himself. They would reach down and tear me to pieces. I closed my eyes.

Something licked my face. The same thick, rough tongue as before. The only thing warm in this frigid waste. I opened my eyes, thinking I'd see some beast with a thousand eyes and teeth the size of Texas waiting to bite into me.

It was a calf. Probably no more than sixty pounds, but it was up and looking at me like I was there to take it home. It was mostly black with a white saddle patch on its back and a white patch over one eye. I'd seen a lot of calves in my time on the farm, and this one looked to be the cutest.

"Well, hello there. What are you doing here?"

"I'm lost," it said.

I scrambled back. The bare ground was slick, so I couldn't get up and run. The calf trotted after me like a puppy.

"Get away from me!"

That made it stop and cock its head to the side. "Aren't you here to help me?" it asked.

I kept scooting back away from it. When my back hit a tree, I stopped. "Cows don't talk. That ain't right. You ain't right. Something is very, very wrong here."

It sat down and watched me for a moment. "I thought you were here to save me." The cow started crying. Actual tears dripped from its big head and shattered on the ground like tiny slivers of ice.

I pulled my knees up to my chest and shook my head. I must've fallen from the stool. That's it. I fell and I hit my head. I'm dreaming all this. This ain't real at all. Cows don't talk and cows don't cry. This is all just some sort of dream.

The calf's cries got louder. "I want to see my momma," it said between wails.

A long, mournful moo came from the woods beyond. I was already cold, but a chill ran down my spine like someone had dropped ice down my shirt. The more the calf cried, the louder the moos became. They didn't sound like momma coming to find this baby. I'd never heard moos come across like wolves, but that's what these sounded like. As if some pack of wolf-cows were on their way to eat this baby.

"Stop that! Stop the crying. Something's coming. Shush."

The calf didn't stop; it kept on wailing. I crawled to it on my hands on knees and hugged it like it was a child in need of comforting.

"Look, stop the crying, I'll help you find your momma."

The crying slowed, and the calf sniffled. "Really? You'll help me find my momma?"

"Yeah, sure thing. Just keep quiet."

This was some kind of dream, so I had to figure a way out of it. I'd had lots of dreams about weird things, but never anything like this before. Maybe it was just a matter of time before I had a dream about talking cows. I had, after all, spent all my life working with them. So, why not?

"I'm going to get my phone. Just stay right here."

My phone sat a few feet away, shining its light up into the air. I grabbed it and tried to call Pa. I got a busy signal, but not the standard busy signal tone. This one instead went, "moo, moo, moo, moo." This dream was getting weirder by the minute.

I hung up the phone and slid it into the pocket of my coveralls. I had to figure out how to wake up from this dream. I closed my eyes and tried to think about waking up. I slapped myself. My cold hand stung hitting my cold cheek. I tried to think about going to the bathroom. Sometimes that'd wake me up.

Nothing worked.

"I want to see my momma," the calf said again.

"Yeah, I got that. I'm trying to get out of here."

A long moo came from somewhere in the trees.

"Oh, no. It's getting closer. You need to get me out of here. Please take me to my momma."

I went back and sat next to the calf as if it'd somehow protect me, a two-hundred-pound grown man. I was more than twice the size of the calf, yet here I was, scared like a little boy at some demon cow out in the woods that I couldn't see. Cows were herbivores. They didn't eat people. Or other cows for that matter.

"Where's your momma?" I asked. I felt stupid talking to a calf. Cows were just big, dumb creatures. They didn't understand anything other than taps to get them to move in the right direction when it was milking time and when it was feeding time.

"I don't know. I thought you were here to take me to her."

"Well, what's that in the woods?"

The thing in the woods mooed again. It was getting closer. I almost had a direction on it. I think. The echo in these woods wasn't like anything I'd heard before. I would have thought there was more than one, but the sound was identical each time I heard it. Had to be an echo.

"Come on, we need to move. I think that thing is coming for us." I started to lead the calf away from the open spot and deeper into the trees.

"I've seen others like me around here. Some have gotten away to see their mommas. I want to get away and see my momma."

"So have you seen those things? Do you know what they are?"

The calf stopped and shook itself off. "They're big and scary. They come for some of us. Carry us away."

That didn't sound good. As freaky as a talking calf was, I had the distinct feeling that whatever made those eerie sounds was far worse. I had to get this little one out of harm's way so I could figure out how to get back to the dairy. I didn't belong in these woods. Heck, I wasn't even sure if the calf belonged in these woods.

The two of us walked along for several minutes before the sound came again. I wrapped my arms around myself, as if that'd somehow protect me from cold chill and the sound.

"Doesn't this cold bother you?" I asked, and gracefully tripped over an exposed root. I got my phone out and in front of me to light the way.

"What do you mean? It's always this temperature." The little calf stopped and its ears perked up.

"What is it?" I tried to listen as well, but I didn't hear anything. Not at first. It started like a distant thud followed by a dragging noise. "Do we need to get out of here?"

"I don't know. I don't know where to go. I just want to see my momma. Please help me!"

I knelt down and scratched the calf between its ears. "It's going to be all right," I wanted to promise the little thing, but I had no idea if things were going to be all right or not. For all I knew I was lying on the floor of the stall with Daisy stomping my brains into jelly and causing me to have this weird dream that would end in a flash.

That's when a bright light swirled from all around.

"What the hell was that?"

The calf nudged closer and knocked me down. "That's the light. I think we need to find the light."

"The light? What are you talking about?"

"Before the others would disappear, there would be a light. Maybe we need to find the light."

Every near-death experience I'd ever heard in my life

warned me to stay away from the light. That was the last place I wanted to go. I was dumb, but I wasn't stupid. I sure wasn't going to follow a calf into the light.

"We're not going into the light. We need to find another way out of here."

A baleful moo sounded from right behind us as another pulse of light lit the area. Off in the distance the biggest cow I'd ever seen reared up on its hind legs. It was far away, but not nearly far enough. I was hopefully mistaken, but I thought the light glimmered off long, dagger-like teeth.

"Let's move." I grabbed the calf by its ear and tugged. It sat down and started crying again. "We do not have time for this. We have got to get moving. What are you doing?"

"I want to see my momma. Please take me to my momma. I don't wanna die."

"Who said anything about dying? Now get up. We have got to get moving."

Light flashed again and the big cow was far closer. I reached down, picked up the calf, and started to run.

It kicked. It bit. It butted me in the head.

"Stop! I can't run with you doing that." It was far heavier than it looked and I stumbled a few times and nearly fell on top of the calf. Finally it twisted its way free and hopped out of my arms. I could hear it crying as it ran away.

"Fine, go then. I was trying to save you. Now I just have to save myself."

I wanted to mean it. I really did. How could I think about saving a calf when I really needed to get out of wherever I had wound up? There had to be some way back. Even if this was some mental game where I needed to wake myself up, I knew I could do it. I couldn't be hurt that badly, could I?

Running in the opposite direction of the calf only lasted for about ten seconds before a flash of bright light caused me to turn around. I saw the big, toothed cow slowly plodding toward the calf. It was going to catch it and eat it, I just knew it was. Maybe that's what this whole mental game was all about: save the calf, save yourself.

The flashes of light came quicker. I pocketed my phone

and hoped I wouldn't trip or hit anything. Twice as I ran toward the calf I had to duck just in time to avoid being brained by a branch. I was getting there faster than the big cow, which, upon closer inspection in the flashes, was covered in blood with patches of skin missing and exposed bone. Its eyes burned brilliant red as it stomped along after the calf.

Even though I was faster than the big heifer, my path was longer and I knew I would just miss the calf if I didn't do something. Stupid thoughts ran through my head. Thoughts of getting drunk with my buddies and four or five of us lining up and shouldering a cow to the ground. It usually got up far more upset than those that didn't go down at all. Those that didn't go down usually ran away. Those that went down got up and came after us. Well, it always seemed like a good idea at the time.

This, however, was another matter altogether. I didn't have my buddies with me. I also didn't have anything to drink. There was no way I would be able to push the thing over while it was moving. If I grabbed a hind leg, I was liable to get kicked upside the head and that wouldn't do anyone any good. I had to make a grab for a front leg and hope the thing overcorrected and fell over.

I came up alongside the cow and reached out for its front leg. Just before I could get a hold of it, the thing stopped. My brain wasn't quick enough to realize just what was going on until I found myself in front of it. The massive cow snorted, lowered its head, and charged. That's when I realized that it knew all along what I'd been planning. Now I had to make up things as I went along.

As it got closer, I jumped into the air. Its head rose up. The mouth opened, filled with hundreds of sharp teeth. It clamped shut, just missing my leg. I landed on its back. Again it stopped and started to buck. My hands gripped on torn flesh, but slipped from all the blood on the beast. I fell off to the side.

The calf had continued to run off. The flashes of light grew brighter and lasted longer. The big cow turned away from me and went after the calf. I kept up my chase as well, but stopped. I needed to have a weapon of some sort if I was going to stop that big, nasty cow. I only had one thing.

My coveralls.

If I took them off, I'd get my clothes dirty. If I didn't, that little calf would suffer and probably die. I had to do what I could to protect it. I unzipped and stepped out of my coveralls and tied one arm to one leg. With my makeshift lasso, I went after it.

In no time, I'd caught up with the vampire cow. I tried to clomp along quieter, but hopefully the thing was stupid enough to think I'd try the same thing again. Instead, I came at it from behind. I watched the rhythm of its rear legs and just as the right hind leg came up, I looped it with my coverall lasso. I stopped and pulled.

The beast let out a horrific moo and started to turn. I had the tiger by the tail. I followed it around and continued to pull its rear leg up as high as I could hold it. When it started to turn in the other direction, I turned to face it, pulling with all my might. The light had stopped flashing and was now as bright as daylight. The cow, with its long teeth, red eyes, and black skin, snorted and snarled.

It couldn't get to me. I had its rear leg pulled at an awkward angle. The more it tried to get at me, the more it lost its balance. Finally the beast fell and hit the ground hard.

I hopped in and did the best I could to tie its two rear legs together before running to catch up with the calf. I was quite out of breath by the time I finally got to it. I didn't know how long the coveralls would hold it, but I hoped it would be long enough.

"It's all right. It's all right. I stopped it. You're going to be all right." My words came between ragged, panting breaths.

The calf collapsed into my arms and wailed in my ear. I held it tightly.

I've never been one to get attached to cows at the dairy. They were working animals. They had a job to do and so did I. Why I was sitting on the ground blubbering with a calf, I have no idea, but I needed to get home. Pa was sure to be wondering just what had happened and I needed to be there.

"You said we needed to go to the light, right?"

The little calf looked up at me. "I think that'll take me to see my momma. That big, mean, cow isn't going to get me and kill me, is it?"

"Not if we get moving. I think the light is just ahead, over there." I helped the calf to its feet. Its legs were shaking from exhaustion, but it only had a little way to go and then we'd be at the light.

A warm wave pushed at us like an invisible hand. I fell to my knees, but quickly got back up.

"What was that?" the calf asked.

"I don't know. Let's just keep going. We're almost there."

Looking into the light hurt. I wasn't sure just how long I'd been in the darkness, but it felt like having a flashlight shoved in your face after sitting in an open field on a cloudy night. I could just make out indistinct shapes.

"Hurry, let's go." Another warm wave hit us and pushed us forward once more. The calf stopped.

"What's my name?" it asked.

"I don't know. Shouldn't you know what your name is?"

"I can't go into the light if I don't know my name. How will my mother know me?"

I rolled my eyes. "Just go. Trust me, she'll know who you are."

"Please, just give me a name."

"Fine. Baby is your name, now go."

The calf tilted its head to the side and shook it. "No, that's not a good name. I need a good name."

"What do you mean a good name? I'm freezing, there's a killer vampire cow after us, and I want to go home. Let's get moving."

"It has to be something better than 'Baby'. Try again."

"Baby...McButter. How's that? You've got a name. Can we go now?"

"I think I like that better. What's your name?"

"That's the least important thing. Now go." I went to give the calf a nudge to get it moving and something pulled my leg out from under me. Teeth, long and sharp, dug into my flesh. I screamed.

"No! Let go!" The little calf hopped onto my back and smashed the nose of the monster with its little hooves.

"Just get out of here. Go!"

The thing continued to pull me backward. I knew it was over. What could I do? Those long fangs were sunk deep into my flesh and there was no way out.

Standing on my back, the calf head butted the monstrosity.

It dropped me. It actually let go. Unfortunately the calf was the next closest target. I kicked the cow in the head, which stopped it for just the moment we needed. I grabbed the calf and started to run.

My leg slipped out from under me. Pain shot up my leg like fire. I got back up and started running once more, doing my best to ignore the shards of pain.

Warm slime covered my face and I closed my eyes and just kept running toward the light. I held the calf close to my chest and ran.

I hit something hard. The ground? My eyes popped open and I drew in a breath. Slimy viscera covered me from head to toe. In my arms I held the little calf with a white patch over its eye. We'd made it out. Somehow I'd gone into a strange world and pulled this calf out with me. It was the most incredible thing that'd ever happened to me. Probably the most incredible thing that would ever happen to me. I had no way I could ever explain it to anyone.

"I done told you to be careful with Daisy, Junior. You wasn't never supposed to go in after a stuck calf." Pa stood next to Daisy, comforting the heifer. She'd suffered a lot during the birthing process. Her breathing appeared strong and she, more than likely, would make it.

"This isn't just a calf," I said, wiping slime from its head. "This is Baby McButter."

A Traveler's Tale

by Christopher Hite

"ID card, please."

"Good morning," Will said, handing his ID to the guard. He grimaced as he glimpsed his photo printed under the Reagan Nuclear Plant company logo on the card. *Bad hair day* barely began to describe it.

The guard glanced at the ID then at Will to confirm the picture match. "Go on through, sir."

Will nodded. "Thanks. Have a good day" He went through the checkpoint, his briefcase almost getting stuck in the turnstile as he made his way to the elevator that led to his second floor office.

He flipped on his terminal as he walked into the office and pulled the sheet off his Dilbert day calendar. Asok had somehow grown a Pinocchio nose in the calendar's cartoon dated April 8th.

While he waited for the terminal to come up, he looked at the picture behind his desk. The picture was of him with his sensei at Defence! Martial Arts Studio on the day he earned his 1st degree black belt; one of the proudest moments of this life.

Will turned back to his terminal and quickly sent a message to the department heads, asking them to meet him in the White Room in five minutes. Then he locked his terminal and left his office. Upon arrival, he found all five nuclear generator technicians, one for each generator, ready to enter the White Room.

The lead technician of the Beta generator spoke up first. "Beta generator has a slight power fluctuation, sir."

"We will have to check that out, then, won't we, Johnson? Any other problems last night?"

"None to report, sir!" the other technicians said in unison.

Will breathed a sigh of relief. Inspections were his least favorite part of the job. Critical, but painful to carry out.

"Well, then, let's get suited up! You all know the drill. When you get out there, check everything and report your generator's status. Remember, no problem is too small."

Once the technicians were suited up, they stepped through the airlock and out of the White Room.

"Let get this over with," Will said to the Alpha generator technician.

He first checked the display of generator Alpha, verifying that all of the automatic alarms were working. That step completed, he carried out the physical inspection and quickly moved on to the Beta generator.

"What do you make of this, sir?" the Beta technician asked. He pointed to the display that still showed the same odd power drain as before.

"Anything obvious?" When the technician shook her head, Will looked at the generator. "All right, let's take a closer look at the equipment to see what is causing this power fluctuation." Will and the technician began to make a physical examination of the system.

"What is going on here?" Will said, pointing at a panel where several screws were missing. "There wasn't any maintenance scheduled for last night, was there?"

"No, sir. Last night should have been fairly routine."

Will moved cautiously. A loose panel might be nothing, but it also could be something very serious. As he leaned closer, he noticed that the panel seemed to be glowing.

"Then why is this panel loose? Bring me the tool set for this generator and then check the overnight logs, would you?"

The technician did as she was told and brought Will the Beta generator's tool set and then checked the overnight logs.

Will laid out the tools for the physical inspection.

"The log doesn't show any physical access to the system, however there is a system alert warning of the increased power levels," the tech said when he returned. "I don't understand it."

"Okay, well, something happened. Let's open this thing up and see what's going on." Will picked up the hex screwdriver and removed the remaining screws.

He pulled the cover panel off and looked inside. "Well, you don't see that every day, now, do you?" Will moved out of the way so that the technician could see. There, inside the panel, was a glowing crystal.

"Chris, take this screwdriver and hand me the notepad." He took notes on the crystal's appearance and relative distance from important pieces of equipment.

"Okay, it isn't touching anything other than the housing here." Will reached toward the crystal. "I'm going to try to remove it now. Before I do, you should monitor my progress from the control room." He waited until the technician had left the area before he grabbed the thing.

The edge of the crystal was sharp and sliced right through the glove. As his skin touched it, there was a bright flash of light and the generators and the entire building faded out until they were partially transparent.

He shielded his eyes from the bright light. But even with his eyes closed, the light burned his eyes.

Blinking back tears and squinting through tortured eyes, the scene before him changed and Will suddenly saw everything all at once.

He watched himself walking in, or rather, out, of the generator room. He saw himself talking with the technicians in the room above as the entire morning spooled out before him in reverse.

Things moved faster as the lighting faded back from daytime levels to evening. Shortly after that something caught his eye: a man dressed in a lab coat walked in and began tampering with the generator.

The man was wearing gloves as he placed the crystal inside the panel of the Beta generator. Then he took off the gloves and touched the crystal, disappearing for a few seconds before reappearing and putting his gloves back on.

It wasn't until the man removed the crystal from the generator that Will got his first clue as to why he was tampering with the generator. As time crawled backward, the man pulled the crystal away, and it became dull and no longer glowed. The man backed away from the generator and left the room.

"I wonder if that's what's causing that power fluctuation in the generator. Maybe it is actually being used as the power source for this crystal," Will thought to himself as he kept moving through time.

There was another bright flash of light and the time stream stopped swirling around him. When he opened his eyes again everything had changed.

"Where the hell am I?" he asked the nearly empty clearing around him. He looked around, trying to find a sign or something that would identify where he was. Eventually, he saw a sign along the road showing an image of the power plant. The sign read, "Future site of the Ronald Reagan Nuclear Power Facility".

"Well, at least I know where I am. The real question now is when?"

Will followed the road away from the empty lot, finally arriving in a small town. At first, he couldn't find any street signs.

He tried to remember his orientation day at the plant. They had given him a little history, but for the life of him, he couldn't remember if the town had been here when the plant was built or if it had come after.

All around him were buildings he didn't recognize: small buildings that were all bunched together: more like a cluster of work huts than a town. What he did recognize was the smell of pizza – the intoxicating smell reminded him that he was famished. Will followed the aroma until he came to a restaurant.

Maybe he could ask for directions when he grabbed a slice. That would give him an idea of when and where he was. He entered the restaurant and grabbed a number from the ticket dispenser at the front door and waited his turn in line at the counter. When the clerk called out his order number, Will approached the counter to order and pay for his food.

"That'll be $1.50."

Will pulled out his wallet and paid the clerk.

The clerk handed Will his pizza and receipt with a smile. "Thank you, have a good day."

As Will left, he and realized he'd forgotten to ask for directions. Luckily, the receipt had the address, and even more telling, the date. It read 4/14/1989.

"Holy crud, I really did time travel." Panic came over him as he tossed the rest of the pizza into the nearest trash can and ran to the nearest street sign.

"Reed Street? Where the heck is that?" It wasn't one he recognized, but then he had never really paid much attention to the little town as he drove through it on his way to work. "Jon Street, now that is one I know!" he said as he came to the next intersection. This was the last road he followed before he arrived at work.

"Great, so I know where I am and I know when I am, but what I don't know is how I am going to get back."

Will approached the street corner and prepared to cross. There wasn't a lot of traffic; either cars or people. That was likely why he saw him. The man on the other side of the road was dressed in a trench coat, sunglasses, and fedora. The oddly overdressed man crossed the street at the same time as Will did and headed right for him. As they crossed paths, Will tried to stay out of his way, but the crosswalk was narrow and the man snagged his arm as he went by, dragging him to the other side of the street and shoving Will against a wall.

"Where is it?" the man hissed in his ear.

"Where is what? I don't know what you...."

"Don't play stupid with me, pal, I know you took it out of the generator. "

The man tried to punch Will in the face, but Will blocked the punch and used a throw that he learned in karate. He successfully took the man to the ground and punched his assailant in the face before he started to run away. Whoever this was, he needed to put some distance between the two of them in case his assailant had a weapon.

As he ran, he felt pain and something warm and wet running down his side.

Will looked down and saw that he'd been stabbed Blood was streaming down his side and cooling quickly. It didn't take long before the blood loss made him feel dizzy.

Time slowed down for Will. As if on cue, a second man in a trench coat and glasses grabbed him and rifled through his pockets. He felt lightheaded and nauseated as he tried to stop his assailant, but he was already too weak. The man dumped him hard on the pavement. Will looked behind him to see this new man running away with the crystal in his gloved hand. The pain became more intense and he collapsed to the ground, clutching his stomach.

Will put his hand across the wound to try to control some of the bleeding. As he did, dust on his shirtsleeve from the crystal fell onto his hand. There was a bright flash of light before he closed his eyes, and everything went black.

Will woke up in a hospital bed feeling slightly dizzy with an ache in his side. He was still alive. He didn't know when or where he was, but at least he was still alive.

The clock on the wall was one of the digital ones that displayed the time and date as well as the weather and humidity. It read 12:30 p.m. Monday, April 8.

"At least it looks like I'm back," he said to himself as he

pushed the call button on the side of his bed. A nurse came in a minute later.

"Oh, good, you're awake! How do you feel?"

"I feel okay. Can you tell me where I am?"

"I'm glad you're feeling better. You are in Mount Sinai Hospital. The doctor wanted to be notified when you woke up. Do you need anything before I do that? Ice? Water?"

Will thought for a moment before responding. "Is it possible for you to leave the code to the locker with me so that I can get my things?"

"Sure, but wouldn't you like me to get them for you?"

"No, I think I can manage."

The nurse checked his IV then handed him the key code. "To use it, just push the pound key, then insert this code."

"Thank you." After she left, Will tried to get out of bed, but quickly discovered how much damage had been done. He sat back down and took several deep breaths before trying again. It took a considerable amount of effort and caused a great deal of pain, but he eventually got back to his feet. Before he made it two steps, he had to sit back down. It was obvious from his weakened state that the pain meds were helping, but not as much as he would have liked. Defeated, he sat and waited a bit before he pushed the button again.

After he retrieved his stuff out of the locker, Will fished his cell phone out of his pocket. As he did this, he felt something inside the left front pocket of his jacket. It was the crystal! What the heck?

Will thought back to his time in the town. The guy in the trench coat took the crystal from him after he was stabbed... didn't he?

Somehow it had come back to him, the last person who used it. Was that how it worked?

Will called the number of the head technician in charge of Beta generator.

"Jamie here."

"Jamie, its Will Stockholm. Have one of your technicians check out the generator for power fluxes."

"Yes, sir." Will heard Jamie put the phone down and yell

across the room, "Johnson! Go check out the generator! I need a report of all power fluxes in the past hour!" There was the sound of the phone being picked up again. "Just a second, sir, I have Johnson looking into it."

"Have him check the last two hours, Jamie."

"Make that two hours!"

Will waited in silence for a few minutes.

"Will, Johnson says there have been no reports of any fluxes since this morning."

"Okay, thanks."

"What happened to you this morning? One minute you were working with Chris on the generator, and the next, you were gone. I know you hate inspections but...."

"It hard to explain. I promise I'll tell you later."

"All right, you're the boss, Boss."

Will hung up, and dialed his boss Greg's number.

"This is Greg."

"Greg, I got hurt this morning on the way in to work. I am going to be out of work for a while."

"Are you all right? Is there anything I can do?"

"No, I am just going to need some time to heal up."

"I got a report from the generator team that you left in the middle of an inspection."

"Yeah, I thought I would be okay, but as it turned out, I was not as well as I thought."

"Okay, well, I hope to see your report on those power fluctuations from last night. And I'm sending you several other reports I need you to work on when you are well enough."

"All right boss, thanks." He turned his phone off and let the pain meds take him back under.

A week later, when he was home from the hospital, he took out the crystal, careful not to let it touch his skin. The thing was beautiful. He hadn't really had a chance to look at it before, but it really was. He felt like he was being drawn into it every time he looked at it. When it was out of his sight, he wanted to be looking at it, touching it. Will memorized it. He learned every crevice and line.

Now that he understood why the crystal had been placed in the generator, he began to figure out a way that he could get it in there again. He could feel the crystal drawing him to the past, and the possibilities that lay there. He could not resist its pull, and knew that he had to do whatever it took to travel again. He would do whatever it took. And no one would be able to stop him.

The Realm of Fire

by Dan Absalonson

Part 1

I knew I was in trouble when my father's men found me hiding in a tree next to the army practice field.

"You must come down at once, Prince Drefan. You are needed in the..."

"Yes, I know. I am supposed to be at my lesson."

"No, Your Highness. You are needed elsewhere. We cannot speak of it here. Please hurry, Sire."

"Of course," I said, dropping down. As I walked, I noticed it was much colder than usual for that time of year. They led me to the wizard's living quarters, a place I seldom visited. As we entered, I saw my father King Eadric, and brother Prince Aethelfrith, standing next to Wizard Nerian's bed. He lay there looking more haggard and thin than I had ever seen him. As I walked up to his bedside to take my place at my father's side, I realized I had not seen the dear wizard in many days.

"Fool boy. Sneaking off like that," my father said.

"I was just..."

"Silence. We have little time and we already wasted some finding you. Listen now. Please tell him Nerian."

I turned to the wizard.

"Tell me what?"

He brushed down the part of his white beard that lay below his lips and spoke.

"I am dying, my prince, and there is no one to replace me as wizard. The kingdom needs you and you must leave soon."

"Where must I go? Tell me and I will leave at once. Why have you not already sent a messenger, Father? Surely there is a rider more skilled than I..."

"Just listen to him, son," Father said, spitting out his words while trying to hold his temper.

The wizard opened his mouth to speak but began coughing instead. He held up his hand. His bone-thin fingers looked like the gnarled branches of a tree, his veins twisting up like roots searching for water. His hacking subsided and he spoke in a feeble voice I had never heard from him before.

"My power is fading. Soon I will pass on, and the kingdom will need a wizard. You, my prince, are the only one who can become one."

"A wizard? You have the wrong man, Nerian. I am to be a soldier. I cannot..."

"Silence, boy! Listen to him," my father barked.

Being a wizard was the last thing I wanted to do. I wanted to lead our army into battle someday with a sword in my hand, not a wizard's staff.

"You must replace me, Prince Drefan. My power is leaving me. The kingdom grows colder every day. There will come a time when I can no longer hold back the great storms of the West from consuming everything. Our people will not survive, only one with royal blood can travel to the Realm of Fire. Your kingdom needs you, Your Highness."

He took a rasping breath, and his eyes softened as he looked at me.

"I am as surprised as you, my prince. I thought that I still had many lifetimes to live before I had to pass on my position and knowledge. You must listen to me."

I looked at my father, thinking that surely it was all a mistake. The implications of what he was saying hit me hard. He was a royal, a prince like me.

Nerian spoke again, pulling me back to the present. "It is said dragons come from the Realm of Fire, though none know how to get there. It is said to be a land wholly different from our own. There is no road that will take you there, no great body of water on which you can sail to its shores. Legend says the only way to get there is through fire."

"Yes, and who in the burnt realm knows what that means?"

"I know what it means, dear boy, and I am the only one in the kingdom who does. I have been there. It is from that realm that my power comes and where yours will come as well."

I almost spoke to protest again, but heeded my father's warning glace.

"Look upon my staff."

I picked up his staff which was resting against his bed. It was much lighter than I had expected. On one end was affixed a long, dark-red claw of some kind. It looked like it had turned that way from age, but I had always known it to be the brightest of reds. It always stood out among the drab colors of Nerian's robes.

"What you are holding, young prince, is…"

"Your fire staff," I said in a whisper.

"Yes. On the top rests the cleaved talon of a great dragon I once faced in my youth. One such as you must face now."

My mind went from curiosity to terror. I felt my heart thump faster in my chest. I looked at the talon on the staff with a new sense of wonder and respect for the old wizard.

"The dragon's talon is the source of power. It has always been bright, but as you can see, its power is now fading. It has lasted me many lifetimes, keeping my body and this kingdom safe, but soon I will pass on and join my friends who have died and left me behind over the years."

The wizard's speech was broken up once again by hacking coughs.

"The orb of finding leads you to sources of magic. There is a tall tree in the middle of the Red Forest. You must get far away from the magic of my staff for the orb to point toward the tree.

Travel east and let the sands of fire in its spherical body guide you to the portal tree. You will need an axe as well, when you get to the portal tree you will see high upon its trunk a great symbol carved into the wood. With any luck, it should still bear a red glow, though I fear it may have nearly faded. Splash some tree-kill potion from my study onto the base of the tree. It will only take a few good blows with a sharp axe to cut the tree down, then cut around the symbol. Take some charcoal and parchment with you to copy the symbol. Be precise, my prince, it must be just as you see it carved into the tree. Once that is done, build a great fire, then cast the piece of wood with the symbol upon it into the flames. This will create a portal to the Realm of Fire."

The wizard stopped, waving his hand toward the glass of water beside his bed. My brother walked over and gave it to him. He took a slow, shallow drink and then gave it back.

"Thank you."

The wizard looked to me again.

"Once you see the fire cloaked in a bright red blanket of power, step into it. You will not be burned. Let us hope there is still enough power left in the symbol I carved upon the tree ages ago to send you through. Once there, you must find a dragon. The bigger they are, the more power they hold. Wait until it slumbers and then sneak upon his den."

The wizard stopped talking to cough something up. He leaned over and spit upon the stone floor, then lay back down and continued.

"It must be a male dragon. They have large horns, while females do not. You will need to chop off the talon from its longest finger then you will need to run for safety. You must leave the realm immediately lest it catch you and kill you.

All the powers of the staff are written in a book I keep in my study. It's bound in a dark leather volume. When you return, you will need to study it well so you can serve your kingdom with its power. Never let it fall into the hands of enemies. I don't have much time left. Soon the power of my staff will run out. The portal will die with me. Now go, my prince."

I wanted to laugh, or cry, or say something to convince them all that this was insanity. Yes, I wanted to be a warrior someday, but how could I face a dragon? A great beast whose kind everyone thought were long dead? They were from legends and fancy tales, not something you could actually go out and find. I could not get any words to come out. To my surprise, my father spoke for me.

"I have known you all my life, Nerian, so I know you would not say these things unless they were of the utmost importance. Would it not be wise for my best men to go with him? I do not wish my son to be put in such danger." The wizard held up one hand as he coughed into another. Once his coughs subsided, he spoke.

"My lord, I wish you could send your entire army with the boy, but the portal will only allow him through – only one with royal blood. That is how the ancients wanted it, so common men could not travel into the realm and capture this great power for themselves."

"Then I will go with him. Surely I can protect him." To my great surprise, my brother spoke. It was the first time I learned he had love for me, for he only showed me pain and embarrassment.

"I fear we cannot put the heir to the throne in such danger, Your Majesty."

With tears in his eyes my father put his hand on Aethelfrith's shoulder.

"Nerian is right, my son. We must keep you safe so the kingdom has someone to take my place when I pass on. We can't risk it. There is no other heir, and your brother is the only other who can journey through this portal our dear wizard speaks of."

My father straightened his robes and stood taller. He cleared his throat, tilted back his crown, and wiped away his tears.

"All those days sneaking off to see the soldiers train might come to your aid now my petulant boy," he said as he looked over at me with a sad but forceful grin on his face.

"Go now to Nerian's study and gather what you need. I'll meet you in the stables with the finest axe the blacksmith has to offer And it's high time I gave you your first sword."

I was barely listening to what my father was saying. It was all I could do to keep the panic from spilling out in hot, messy tears. My breaths were heavy and my ears felt as though they were stuffed with cotton, but when my father said the word *sword*, I came out of it.

"Wait, I finally get a sword? I will go on this journey and become a wizard as long as I get to keep the sword."

"That's a big surprise," my brother said.

"That is the son I know. May it bring you courage my, boy. Now go!"

Part 2

In the wizard's study, which was a dark and musty chamber, there were bound books and scrolls everywhere. For the first time, I wondered if I would ever find the love for reading that he had. I doubted he had any tales of heroes going on adventures in his dusty tomes. I walked over to his desk where a great many books were piled next to his broad pipe. Above the desks were shelves with more books. Between a set of dark blue and faded green book spines sat an orb upon a black blanket. I took it down from the shelf and gazed into it. Inside the glass was red sand. It clung to the side of the orb facing the wizard's bedchamber where his staff leaned against his bed. Some mysterious force was pulling the sand toward the nearest source of magic. It took a great effort to stop looking at the orb, but I tore my eyes away from it. I took one final look around the study wondering if I would ever return to it and claim it as my own, and then set off toward the stables.

My father was there with my brother. A strong horse named Fristle, who was white with brown spots, was saddled up with a bedroll and pack strapped to his back.

My father was holding a handsome sword that looked small in his hands.

"Here, my boy," he said handing it to me.

The blacksmith said it will do well in your hands. It was made with a reduced length, but hold it out."

I did, swinging it around the way I saw the soldiers do it when I watched them from my tree.

"Yes, that sword fits you well. I see you don't have trouble handling its weight. That is good."

I held it up and turned it over. It was the most beautiful thing I had ever seen, and it was mine.

"Thank you, Father. I will cherish this blade."

My father laughed.

"I know you will. Now put this sheath on and put it away before you run off to court the thing."

My brother laughed, but it wasn't his usual cruel laugh. I looked over at him. He held an axe for me. I put the sheath on my back and slid the sword where it belonged. I looked up and my eyes met my brother's.

"It looks good on you," he said. I had never before seen the sincere look that was upon his face in that moment. "Please come back to us. I know I give you nothing but trouble and bruises, but you are my brother and I do love you. Return home safely to us. Use that sword well. Be the hero you've always dreamed of being, and come back so that someday we can rule this land together. I wish I could go with you and protect you, but this is your quest. May this axe fell the great tree swiftly, Be careful, it has been sharpened well. I love you, brother."

He handed the axe to me. I was surprised to see him acting this way, but it also warmed my heart to see that he truly cared for me. It just took a journey likely to end in my death for him to tell me.

"Thank you, Aethelfrith. I love you too, brother."

"Make me proud, son, and please come back to us. Your mother needs you. Your brother and I need you. Most of all, your kingdom needs you. Return with power of the dragons and help us rule over this land with the protection of your magic for another age. We're all counting on you, son."

He grabbed my brother and pulled him in close.

"Make us proud."

The tears were in his eyes again. He pulled me in, and we embraced. Then he let go of my brother and took me by the shoulders. He looked me up and down.

My father drew us both in again, and then waved his hand toward my horse. I climbed into the saddle and looked down at them.

"There is some food in your pack, warm blankets, and the parchment and charcoal you'll need. Stay safe, my son. Return to us."

"I will," I heard come from my mouth.

I tried not to think about the danger before me and bid them farewell. I rode out of the castle, through the gate of the outer battlements, and on to the East Road.

I rode for a long time; until I could tell Fristle was tired. I hopped off of him and led him to a stream. While he drank, I pulled the orb of finding out of my pack. The crimson sand inside was no longer pressing against the glass toward the castle. Now it was pointing me east toward the forest.

"We're getting closer, Fristle!" I said.

He blew out some air in a dismissive way. I envied his ignorance of the danger we were riding toward. Then I corrected myself. He was not going toward danger, I was going toward danger. I put the orb away and unsheathed my sword. I hoped that looking at it would replace my growing fear with the joy of holding my own sword. It did feel amazing just pulling it from my back. It worked for a few seconds. It was such a beautiful blade, but I couldn't stop thinking about facing a dragon for long.

Once Fristle had rested and eaten his fill of the grass around us, we continued east. Soon, the meager landscape of rolling hills was replaced by tall, thick trees, and the wind blew stronger at the higher elevation, making the branches of the trees look like great hairy arms beckoning me into the forest.

They swayed, sounding like a multitude of voices whispering secrets of the magic within. As we left the meadow, the dark, dense forest surrounded us, swallowing up the comforting heat of the sun. I shivered in my saddle and focused my eyes, trying to look for a trail as my vision adjusted to the shade. The trees gave off a strong, fresh smell. I turned around and reached into my pack for the orb of finding.

As I held it before me, the sand inside looked much brighter than it had in the sunlight. It pushed toward the glass in one large clump, directing me further into the forest. I rode on at a slow pace, letting Fristle picking his way through tall foliage, massive rocks, and fallen trees. I kept my left hand on the saddle horn as my right held up the orb. The sand began to shift to the left. I turned Fristle until it once again clung to the glass directly away from us. We continued on like that for a long time.

As night began to fall, I hopped off of Fristle, let him rest and eat again, then we made our way further into the forest. Just when I thought I should stop to make camp and continue our quest in the morning, I noticed the sand had become more violent. Each grain pressed past the others in waves against the glass trying to get closer to the magical source.

As we rode on, the sand began to glow slightly. I might not have noticed if the forest had not been so dark, though the trees grew farther apart and our path was easier to traverse. I pushed my heels into Fristle's sides, urging my tired horse to transition from a trot to a canter. I posted, standing in the saddle. My stomach and back were tired and my legs began to burn, but I wanted to find that tree. As scared as I was, I wanted to see the magic symbol and the portal.

Then the sand shifted, racing back toward me. I stopped Fristle and looked behind us. We had been moving fast and must have passed it.

Turning around, we walked back the way we had come. The only thing I could see were sparse patches of sunlight shooting through the branches. The sand in the orb was clumped up at the top of the glass. I looked up but didn't see anything at first. After a moment, I thought I saw the smallest glimmer of red.

I got off of Fristle, walked up to the trunk of the tree, and looked up. There was a faint red glow a long way up through the branches. I retrieved my axe, then led Fristle to a tree a few paces away, tied him to it, and got to work.

I took out Nerian's potion and splashed it across the tree. It ate away the trunk with an appetite spreading a rough cut through the wood. Smoke rose into the air like pungent, curling locks of aged gray hair. It reminded me of Nerian's hair and I wondered if he was still alive. Once the smoke cleared, I poured the remaining potion into the tree, pushing the cut farther in past the center. It went almost all the way through. The great tree teetered, making loud cracking sounds. I hefted the axe. It took only four swings from the other side to send the tree crashing to the forest floor.

I ran toward the top of the tree where the strange symbol was carved. I wondered at the way its form glowed red from magic wielded upon it ages ago.

"Fristle, these dragons must be powerful if one of their fingers contains magic that lasts like this through the ages."

He snorted again as if to say he was the most powerful beast in all the land. I ran to him and got the parchment and charcoal from my pack. Then I went back to the symbol and began copying each line and curve with great care. My heavy fingers took more coaxing to move as they were sore from swinging the axe. It took me a while, but that was okay. I didn't want to find out what would happen if I had one of the markings off when I was on the other side of the portal trying to get back home.

With my work finished, I looked back and forth from the glowing symbol to the parchment. For once, I was thankful for my lessons. I rolled the parchment up and walked back to my horse, securing the drawing in my pack.

I got to work chopping wood until there was enough for a great fire. I cut around the symbol and placed it safely next to

Fristle. I stacked log upon log until I had constructed an enormous cone of wood ready to burn. Beneath, I slid many small pieces of wood and handfuls of dry grass. With my tinderbox, I set the grass and wood aflame. First came smoke, then small flames, and after a time they reached high above my head like great dancing spirits.

The heat was more intense than I could have imagined. I picked up the big chunk of wood with the symbol on it, hoping the wizard was right, and threw it into the fire.

As I watched the flames flicker and sway, the heat of the fire diminished and a red glow began to encompass it. Not knowing how long I would be or if I would ever return, I ran over to Fristle and untied his rope so he could return home even if I never did. All the while, I kept glancing at the fire hoping its red glow would stay strong. As soon as my horse was free, I turned to the red glowing flames, screamed for courage, and ran.

Part 3

I ran toward the cold flame. It was big and bright and colder than the darkest night of winter. I shivered. My limbs felt numb. I kept running. The red consumed me. It was all. Nothing had ever been but the red glow. My eyes were shut tight, but the red shined through. Then I felt warmth returning to my body and the bright light began to fade. I opened my eyes. I was in the Realm of Fire.

The air was still. The red and cold faded away, and then a great gust of air blew me onto my back. I heard what sounded like an enormous tent being erected, or perhaps a flag the size of our castle flapping in the wind. I sat up and looked to the heavens. It was a dragon. A huge dragon with great horns.

I looked around for shelter, not wanting to become supper for the beast. Behind me was a massive boulder. I got up and scrambled behind it. I waited until I could hear that he had flown well past me. I could tell he was not close to me anymore. When I poked my head around the rock, I still expected him to dive for me, but he was a dark shape in the distance.

I looked around at the strange place I had been spit into. Everything was red. The rocks were gray, with a red hue. The leaves of the trees were maroon. The sky was like a big wash of crimson paint, sprinkled about with sprays of auburn rain clouds. Suddenly my lesson room back at the castle didn't seem so gloomy now.

Yes, I finally had a sword, an axe, and a magic talisman, but it looked like I had been dropped into hell and now I had to find a dragon.

I started walking in the direction the beast had gone. I could still see his dark form flapping in the distance. He flew left toward a mountain that blocked him from my view.

Despite being more tired than I had ever been, I kept walking. I wondered how soldiers could march all day with weapons strapped to their bodies.

As I trudged on, I started to lose hope of finding the dragon. He had passed out of my view and there was no way I could keep up with him. I kept my eyes to the sky in hopes of finding another one while also not wanting to see one again for as long as I lived.

Eventually, I crested a hill and the side of a great mountain came into view. I could see smoke coming from a huge cave which sat a long way up the mountain. It looked like someone had constructed a fire as big as my portal flame and that a giant was blowing its smoke out into the sky. A great plume of smoke floated out from the cave and then up into the air to join with the reddish clouds. I thought that must be where the dragon had gone.

I continued on to the mountain, and began my ascent. After walking for a while, it became too steep to stay on my legs. The axe and sword strapped to my back felt like great hands reaching up to pull me away from the mountain. I leaned forward and began to climb on my hands and knees. It was steep, but there were plenty of trees and rocks, which supplied me with secure hand and footholds. And so I kept climbing.

Though I was sweating from the exertion, I noticed it was

getting colder the farther I climbed. The air felt thinner and the smell of something like rotten eggs was beginning to bother me. The higher I climbed, the stronger it became. Soon, I felt like I was climbing up the cracked side of a massive rotten egg, its spoiled yolk spilling into my nostrils with each deep and labored breath.

My arms and legs ached as I reached a ridge. I stopped and turned to see the view my progress up the mountain had afforded me. I had come a long way. From this vantage, the trees and rocks that had been my guide all seemed to be pointing away from me toward the base of the mountain like friends beckoning me to stop my deadly quest and climb back down to safety. To my right, the hill that had blocked my view of the dragon and taken me forever to walk over now looked like a tiny bump in the vast red landscape.

I held my breath to listen for the dragon. I could barely hear his breathing farther up the mountain; slow and even. I hoped that meant he was asleep. The smell was much worse and I could feel heat coming from above me. I kept climbing.

When it sounded like the dragon was only an arm's reach away, I gripped a rock and pulled myself up to a flat area.

In front of me was the cave and bright red patches of the dragon's scales obscured by the smoke pouring out of his nostrils in great bursts with each exhalation. He was much bigger than I had imagined, bigger than my mind or courage could handle. I lowered myself back down and turned my back to him.

There was no way I was going right up to that thing and chopping one of his talons off without waking him, not to mention getting away alive.

My body was shaking. I pulled out my sword and looked at it for courage. I thought to myself, *What had I always wanted to be*? A brave warrior or someone who faced the enemy and charged forward? I put my sword back, turned around, and started climbing. I made it to the mouth of the cave, my body still shaking.

I tried to make each footstep lighter than the last as a got closer to the great beast. I pulled out my axe, knowing I would have to do it before I lost my courage or I would never be able to get it done. Nerian had said dragons were deep sleepers and he was knowledgeable in all things so with my last ounce of courage, I stopped trying to be quiet and ran.

I came into the dark cave. The smoke was thick and putrid. I kept running through the haze toward the red scales shifting up and down. I could see one of his paws stretched out on the ground just at the edge of the light from behind me.

I raised my axe, not daring to look at the dragon's head, fearing one look would send me running back down the mountain. I came upon the massive hand. The fingers were the size of my legs and the talons, curling out like daggers, spanned the length of my forearm.

Just as Nerian had said, above the talon, the thick scales stopped and there was a thin ring of soft, red dragon flesh. I brought the axe down with all my might. I struck it in the right spot and my axe did its work, slicing through the tip of the dragon's finger and bouncing off the hard stone floor of the cave.

The dragon's head shot up. Its eyes and mouth opened, then it let out a deafening howl that made me jump back.

I dropped the axe, peed myself, grabbed the massive red talon, and ran. I could feel the dragon's mighty body crawling toward me through the shaking ground. When I was close to the edge of the plateau, I looked back. He was right behind me. I don't know what I was thinking or why I did it, but I saw a tree branch and jumped for it.

I flew over the steep slope of the mountainside and landed just above the tree branch I was aiming for as if the tree had caught me. I tried to drop down, but my pack was stuck in the branches. I got one arm out of a strap, but the other was stuck tight. I panicked and pulled as hard as I could, but it wouldn't move.

I reached up and unsheathed the sword. I slid it between my shoulder and the strap then pushed. My sword cut through and I fell past the branch I wanted to land on to a thinner one much farther below. Once again the tree caught me.

I felt a brilliant heat press down on me from above. I looked up and saw the tree and my pack on fire. I didn't know what I was going to do, but I still didn't want to die, so I scrambled down the tree as fast as I could. I made it back down to the blessed earth and looked for a hiding place. I didn't want to go down because I had to move fast, and I was afraid I would trip and fall to my death, so I headed across the steep incline. I looked up and saw the dragon circling back around to try and find me. I kept running.

Part 4

As I ran, I spotted a thick patch of shrubbery. I dove into its mess of branches and let them pull in around me. I lay low to the ground, smelling the red earth up close for the first time. It smelled similar to the dirt of my world, but somehow more red, like cinnamon. I remained still and listened. It was easy to hear where the dragon was, for his massive wings beat the air in enormous arcs, sending thunderous sounds my way. For a time, it flew all around the mountain, staying near my elevation. Then it started flying farther down the mountain. I didn't want to risk getting eaten or burned to death, so I stayed hidden in the itchy arms of those thick bushes. Finally, I could hear his wings flapping no more. It was only then that I remembered the parchment with the symbol I needed to get home was inside my pack and now it was all just black ash destroyed by the dragon's breath.

I sat up and raised myself to a crouch. My head popped above the top of the bushes. I looked around. I listened.

The dragon was nowhere to be found. Somehow I had survived. I felt a sense of relief, but with death no longer so close, my mind was able to think again.

My pack. The symbol on the parchment. They were gone. I might as well have been eaten or burned. Now I had no way of getting back to my family. To my home. I stood and crawled out of the bushes, brushing small, broken pieces of it off of me. I collapsed to the dirt and cried until there was a tiny puddle of mud beneath my face. I sat up, sniffed, wiped my nose, felt sorry for myself, and cried some more.

I was doomed to die in the desolate land of red. The place of dragons, scorched earth, and crimson skies. The Realm of Fire.

I wanted to lie back down and die. I wished the dragon had killed me. At least then I wouldn't have to starve to death, wandering around in a blood-red world devoid of all comfort, knowing that I failed everyone I loved and the kingdom I was born to protect.

I looked at the dragon's talon. It was longer than my forearm and about as wide as my wrist at its base. It was a deep shiny red color that seemed to pull your eyes toward it as you looked at it.

Still crying, I began tracing lines in the dirt with the talon. They glowed red for a moment, drying up the bit of mud from my tears and then they were just lines in the sand.

I stopped and looked at the talon and thought hard about what the symbol looked like. Then I began drawing it in the dirt. The red glow clung to the ground with each line I drew and then slowly faded away. I kept working. When I couldn't remember what line came next, I closed my eyes and pictured myself, sitting on the tree with my back against the mountain, holding the parchment, and then it would come to me. I finished the symbol. The freshest red lines in the dirt were glowing, but disappeared moments later. The symbol was just lines drawn in the dirt. I studied it, giving it my full attention. My tutor would have been proud. It looked right, but the magic left its mark and then vanished. I was about to wipe it away when I remembered there was one last line curving off the bottom right of the symbol.

I put the talon to the ground and drew the line with all the precision I could render from my tired hands.

A bright red glow, much brighter than Nerian's symbol in the tree, shone with such brilliance I wiped it away fearing it would draw the attention of the dragon. I stood up and made my way back up to the dragon's cave. When he returned, I would be ready for him, and his deadly burning breath would bring me home.

The smell in the cave was still strong and foul, but I stuck to my purpose; this was my only way home. I turned around and ran to the ledge, then jumped to the tree where my pack once hung. I landed on the tree. Dark burnt bark was above and below me, but the tree was still strong enough to hold me. I held the talon tightly and began to carve into the blackened wood.

As I did, it spread intense red lines. The lines stood out in stark contrast to the blackened tree and, as in the dirt, they faded after a while. But I kept working.

A breeze started up as I worked. I was concentrating so hard to get all the lines right that I didn't notice I could smell the dragon's breath until it was quite strong. He was coming. I kept carving while he flew closer.

The tree began to bend from his powerful, flapping wings. I had to grab the trunk to keep from falling off, but I kept carving. I had three lines left. The tree swayed so much it made my stomach turn. I grimaced and closed my eyes, gripping the tree hard. The dragon flew past the tree and landed in front of his cave. I drew another line.

The tree swayed again. I fought against the urge to vomit. My stomach felt as though it were rolling around inside of me. The tree bent back and stood still for a moment, so I drew another line. I was flung forward again. I held on tightly and looked behind me. The dragon was stomping toward me, his chest growing as he took in a large breath. The tree paused in its violent swinging. I drew the last line. The symbol lit up; every line glowed with a blinding red light. The tree took me for another ride, paused, and then started bringing me toward the mountain again. I let go.

My body flew toward the mountain, thrown from the tree's branches like a stone shot from a sling. I hit the thick bushes and felt the wind go out of my lungs. I pulled my arms up to my face to block the fierce heat of the dragon's immense blast of fire as it devoured the tree. The heat was painful. I thought for sure that I was being burned alive, though the flames did not touch me.

While I was working to catch my breath, I saw the flames being engulfed by the majestic red cold of the magic.

It looked like a giant tree carved out of brilliant ruby shining against the drab maroon sky. I tried to stand, but my legs gave out. They hurt, but I didn't think they were broken. I stood up, clutching the talon, and forced my legs to carry me off the mountain. Everything around me had been red this whole time but now the enormous tree was causing the rest of the world to disappear into its ever-reaching crimson branches.

I stumbled forward, tripped on a rock, and fell into the portal. The cold enveloped me again. My legs stopped hurting and I couldn't feel anything anymore.

The cold expelled me from its bright glow. I fell onto the gloriously brown dirt. I looked up and saw the green trees. I had never loved the color green so much. Past their wonderfully dull branches, the sky was a pale blue.

I must have fallen asleep, because the next thing I remember was my horse blowing air through his lips as if to say, "Hey, wake up and look at me! I'm more interesting than those trees up there."

Fristle had not left. I was so happy to see him. I got up, bone weary and sore, and hobbled over to my horse, with the red talon in my hand, and hugged his neck. Somehow, I made it into the saddle. I rode home for the last time as a prince to become a royal wizard for ages to come.

The Plumbers Portal

by Julayne Hughes

I absolutely was not going to be one of those.

So I pulled my pants up as high as they would go and tightened my belt. Wrench in hand, I lowered myself to my knees on the solid hardwood in front of the open cabinet door beneath my kitchen sink. The water pipes glittered as if daring me to try to repair them.

"I'll fix you, my pretty!" I muttered, then chuckled at my own little joke. It was a bad joke, but hey, I thought it was funny. There was nobody else around who could have laughed anyway, so it didn't matter.

I reached behind me to make sure my pants were still well in place. They'd slipped down some, but not enough to put me in the ranks of one of those kinds of plumbers. I was still decently covered.

I am proud to say that though I don't have much plumbing experience, I am always well dressed. I don't go in for Armani suits or anything like that, but I like to dress in style. Even when I'm working, I like to look better than someone who should be featured on the People of Stuffmart website.

Even more important, I like to make sure I'm sufficiently clothed on the rare occasions I have to fix plugged drain pipes. My kids take excellent (I might say unfair) advantage of the excuses they already have to make fun of me. I'm not about to give them another. Never mind that no child should ever see Dad in any state of undress, however minor.

Anyway, there I was, under the sink, about to tackle the latest plumbing project. One last pat ensured I was, well, decent. I reached toward the offending pipe with the wrench.

I'm not sure what exactly happened. Maybe it was merely a wardrobe malfunction. Whatever it was, let's just say that I felt a healthy breeze in a place that I should not have. In a panic, I dropped the wrench and tried to pull my pants back up where they belonged. That desperate move pitched me forward and I hit my head hard on the pipe.

"Ouch!"

That and a few other choice utterances left my lips.

I kneeled there for a while, waiting for the space to stop spinning. I'd hit my head a few times in my life, and I knew that if I just sat there for a bit, I'd regain my equilibrium and go on with life, albeit with somewhat of a goose egg on my noggin.

Gradually, everything stopped whirling and I gingerly backed out from underneath the sink. My knees hurt from the gray stone floor they pressed against.

Stone floor? My kitchen had a hardwood floor.

"So did you find it?" a woman's voice screeched. Maybe it wasn't technically a screech, but considering the tender state of my head, it sure felt like one.

"Find what?" I mumbled. I struggled to a standing position. I felt feminine hands helping me up. Or *roughly pulling me up* might be a better description.

"My ring, you idiot!" The voice was right in my ear. Now it sounded more like a shriek than a screech. Yes, there is a difference. "What do you think you're under there for? Your health?"

I was still so disoriented that I could just gape and mutter, "Umm."

I was staring at a woman I'd never seen before. Worse, I was standing in a kitchen I'd never been in before.

She rattled on in that annoying voice. "I know your type. You won't find anything and then you'll still charge an arm and a leg. You plumbers are all the same."

She gave me a hard smack in the arm. Ouch!

Great. Now my head and my arm hurt.

"Now get back to work!" she barked. "And pull your pants up!" She whirled and left the room.

I leaned back against the counter, trying to figure out what had just happened. That I was not in my own kitchen was plain. I rubbed my bruised arm, then raised a hand to the growing bump on my head. Everything seemed too real to be a dream. I glared at the pipes under the sink as if this were all their fault. Then I realized something even worse. My hands raced to my waistline.

Darn it! I was now one of those! I adjusted my pants a few inches upward.

I had to figure out how to get back to my own kitchen. I tried to reconstruct events mentally, but the lump on my head made it difficult. It ached even more just thinking about it.

Well, whatever had happened had happened while I was under the sink, so I figured that reenacting my physical position might be my best bet. I knelt on the unforgiving floor and waited.

Nothing happened. My knees protested their proximity to the gray stone floor that refused to change. My throbbing head reminded me of one other thing that had happened to bring me here, but I wasn't keen to recreate that particular part of the experience. At least I could take some small comfort in the fact that I was now decently dressed. Until . . .

Wardrobe malfunction.

Grab pants.

Hit head on the pipe.

After the world stopped spinning, I noticed my knees were no longer protesting. One look down told me why. I had never realized before just how much softer linoleum was than stone. I relaxed into it almost as if it were a cushion. Squares and rectangles formed a plastic pattern that trailed away into the distance.

"Why don't you do that the rest of the way, honey?" said a low female voice. The tone of this one was a stark contrast from the caterwauling that had assaulted my ears a few minutes ago. This voice was almost a whisper. "Let me help you with that."

As if the embarrassment of an exposed inch of backside weren't enough, I suffered the indignity of hands that weren't my own attempting to widen the gap. Instinctively, I batted the hands away and crept out of the compartment.

I sat down on the linoleum and found myself face to face with the second most gorgeous woman I'd ever met. Next to my wife, of course. Those insistent hands wrapped themselves around my throbbing head and pulled it toward lips that were puckering for a . . .

Desperately, I wrenched myself from her grasp and dove under the sink. Now, what was it I needed to do? Oh, yeah.

Wardrobe malfunction.

Grab pants.

Hit head on the pipe.

This time when I regained my equilibrium, I was kneeling on concrete. My poor knees discovered it wasn't any more forgiving than the gray stone had been. A dog was growling somewhere behind me. I could hear rattling. I peeked under my arm and saw a huge specimen of canine on a chained leash. Said leash was attached to a leg of a dining table. The dog barked as if it were sounding an alarm for people miles away, and lunged wildly against its leash. I froze in place.

Now, I don't hate dogs. Some of the smaller ones are kind of cute, particularly when they are sleeping. I suppose I'm more of a cat person, though allergies at our house have precluded our getting any kind of dander-producing animal. But this was no small dog. And it definitely wasn't sleeping. I was sure that those fangs were at least two inches long. And was that bit of leather on the leash fraying? Was the tear getting bigger with each leap? I didn't want to wait around to find out. The dog's barks grew so loud and so frequent that the animal seemed to be roaring like some kind of dragon. There was only one thing to do. Dive.

Wardrobe malfunction.

Grab pants.

Hit head on the pipe.

The roaring continued. But the clamor of barks and growls gradually shifted to blowing wind and pelting rain. It got louder until the winds shrieked like a banshee and the rain assumed deluge proportions. I peeked around the kitchen and found it was fairly dark, but mercifully empty. And thankfully dry, despite the flood that seemed to be gathering somewhere close. There didn't seem to be anybody around. It was perfectly still.

But the same could not be said about the outside. I got to my feet and looked out a window. Or tried to. The sheet of plywood that was over the pane made it difficult to see out. The other windows were all the same. No wonder it was dark.

Now that I thought about it, I guess I remembered hearing weather reports about the huge hurricane that was supposed to make landfall on the Gulf Coast right about...I pulled my phone out of my pocket and looked at the date...now. Time to panic!

Wait a minute, I told myself. This was ridiculous. My home was nowhere near the Gulf Coast, or any other coast, for that matter, unless the fishing hole near my house counted. There were never any hurricanes in the landlocked Midwestern state where I lived. This could not be happening. I must have really hit my head hard.

I heard a crash. My heart jumped into my throat and pounded fiercely. Some part of me wondered why the house was still intact. The building shook as if it were struggling to stand its ground. A deep, thunderous boom made me look toward the ceiling. Cracks spread rapidly along its edges and connected to other fractures like a spider web. Images of hurricanes blowing the roofs off houses sprang to my mind. This was definitely a place I didn't want to be. There was no time to waste. Dive.

Wardrobe malfunction.

Grab pants.

Hit head on the pipe.

This time, the floor was made of tile. Better than concrete, but not by much. There was a sea of legs and a bustle of activity all around me. I could hear shouts and responses.

"Eggs over easy with bacon and white toast!"

"Order up!"

"Plumber done with that sink yet?"

"Sausage gravy with an extra biscuit!"

"Hey, Frank, where's my home fries?"

"Coming right up!"

It wasn't a life-threatening hurricane, but I was getting out of here nonetheless. The shouts faded as I went through the now-familiar routine.

Before I got my bearings again, I felt strong hands lifting me up and out from under the kitchen sink. I had no idea what kind of floor I was now standing on, but this certainly wasn't my kitchen. A large, balding man stood before me, laughing.

When my vision cleared, I could see he wore a blue work shirt that sported a patch on its left shoulder that said, "Pat's Plumbing."

His mirth began to subside. "Welcome to the fraternity!" He smiled at me as if we shared some secret.

"Fraternity?" I said.

He stretched out his hand and I instinctively reached out to shake it. He did something funny with his fingers on my palm that felt almost like water draining. What was that supposed to be? Some kind of secret handshake?

I had a feeling that this guy might have some answers about what I'd just experienced in the last little while, but I wasn't about to waste time getting details. Who knew what else lay in wait for me here? I did not want to know.

I made a move for the space under the sink.

"Wait a minute," the Pat's Plumbing dude said. "Don't you

want an explanation of what just happened? It's only your first time...."

First time? Did that mean there would be others? A wave of panic rose in me as my mind went wild with images of what awful things might be waiting for me underneath other sinks.

I didn't wait another second. I gave my pants a yank downward, then back up. My head hit the pipe and when the world stopped spinning, I finally found myself on the nice, comfortable hardwood of my own kitchen floor.

I rocked backward on my heels and sat down so I could think a minute.

I suppose it was possible that I had stumbled onto some kind of plumber's portal. Maybe lots of people went to fabulous places that way. Perhaps it was just a matter of experimenting and figuring out how to get around.

The prospect didn't look inviting to me. Conk myself on the head? On purpose? So I could land in God knows whose kitchen? Not to mention the complete lack of propriety it required as far as wardrobe was concerned. It went against everything I believed about being properly dressed. I was absolutely not going to be one of those. I kept repeating that to myself silently as if doing so would make it more true.

And what if I got lost? I knew plumbers' unions were pretty powerful, but I couldn't imagine they had some sort of Portal Posse that would come after you if you didn't show up after a while.

I swallowed hard and tried to think things through despite how unbelievable it seemed. After a while, it began to make a strange sort of sense. I had never understood why an entire profession of people did their work with their pants halfway down their...well, you know. Even leaning over with the weight of a heavy tool belt around the waist couldn't explain everything. I think I also now understood the ridiculous amount of time it always seemed to take plumbers to do simple jobs. They were out portal hopping! Then they charged the customer for the time, of course.

I slowly made my way up from the floor and gave my

pants a good, hard tug. I tightened my belt within an inch of its life. These puppies weren't going anywhere. Then I carefully lowered myself again to fix the drain. Once I finished, I put my tools away, took something for my poor aching head, and sat down to rest.

When my head heals up, I might eventually go back and try to navigate the Plumber's Portal. But for the time being, if I have to do something under the sink again, I think I'll wear one-piece overalls.

Finding Olympus

by Jeffrey Hite

Olympus, Near Sun up (Today)

This was not what Rob had expected when he had agreed to come up here with Larry. "Look, we were trying to help, you know."

The sprite and the beast ignored him, as they had they last twenty times he had tried to speak to them. The sprite, which was incredibly strong considering its size, held his arm in place while the beast attached the massive chain to the cliff wall behind him.

"We didn't do anything! We were just trying to help. He is mad with power, you know." He didn't know if he believed any of it, but he had to try.

"It is no use, Rob. They've been sworn to him for millennia. Besides, the big one is deaf." Larry said from beside him.

"Great. Now you tell me. What are they going to do to us?"

"Leave us here."

The giant old man on the other side of him said, "Not to worry, young one. You won't have to wait too long. The sun will be up soon."

Olympus, Midnight – First New Moon of Spring - (Ten Years Before)

Nikoleta looked down over the edge of the cliff and shivered as the wind blew over her. It'd been so long since she called him that, she wondered if he had actually heard her over the howling wind. She thought about calling again, but he had looked up at her when she had said his name the first time. Nikoleta had been around the old gods long enough to know that they would speak when they were good and ready. Calling him again would just annoy him, and possibly make him take longer to answer. But, she did wish he would hurry up; the wind here on the cliff edge was freezing.

"What is it that you want, girl?" he said, finally.

"Prometheus."

"Go away."

"Wait, Prometheus."

"Go away. If I don't rest, my liver will not grow back. If my liver does not grow back...."

"Prometheus, I need to know how you did it," she interrupted him.

"If it does not grow back," he continued as if she had not spoken, "the eagle will rip and tear at my flesh."

"I need your help, I need to know how you got away from Olympus."

"It cannot kill me, but it can torture me, and make me bleed from a thousand places. Then, when it returns the next day it will be hungrier than normal, and even my fully formed liver will not sate its hunger, and again it will attack me and torture me." He paused for the first time and shuttered. "Do you know how long it will take me to heal from those injuries?"

She didn't answer. This was not what she had come to talk to him about. She let him finish speaking, figuring that if she didn't interrupt him, she could convince him to talk about what she wanted. She knew showing proper respect went a long way with the older gods.

"Prometheus," she said when he finally stopped speaking. "I need to know how you got away from Olympus."

"What do you mean, girl? Can't you see I am not going anywhere?" He moved his arm slightly, jingling the huge chains connecting him to the cliff face. "I've been here forever."

"Not forever, Prometheus. A long time, but not forever."

"Stop! I will not hear of the time before."

"You must. You are the only one."

"There was nothing before this."

"Prometheus, you know that's not true," Nikoleta begged.

"There was nothing before this." There was a long silence that followed.

Nikoleta thought about leaving. She thought about giving up, but in her nearly three thousand years of captivity on Olympus, the one thing that she had learned was patience. But the time to wait was over.

Her whole life had been about waiting. Waiting until your power had so diminished that you simply disappeared. Even Hades had been losing his grip; letting the humans recover people that had been dead, by means of so-called medical science.

No, she would not give up. This was the only way that she could turn things around. She was Nikoleta, the final child of mighty Zeus and Hera. The last of the gods born since the humans had relegated Olympus to a place of the past.

Finally, Prometheus did move. He tilted his head up so that he could see her. She tried to push her long hair out of her face so that he might see who she was.

"You have more patience than most."

"Yes, a blessing and a curse."

"Why have you come?"

"I need to talk to you. I need to know...."

"Come down here," he said cutting her off.

"What?"

"You heard me. Don't waste my time. I have enough pain. Come down here so I might see you when I talk to you."

With more than a little trepidation, she stood and

lowered herself over the cliff's edge. She found well-worn foot and handholds that led down to where he hung on the side of the cliff.

"That is better. Now I can see you. Who are you?"

"I am Nikoleta."

"Nikoleta." He rolled her name out and even with his broken voice it sounded nice. "I have not heard of you."

"I am Hercules' younger half-sister." She hoped the memory of the great hero who had once liberated the titan would give her some credence with him without reminding him of her father, who had put him here in the first place.

"Ah, then a daughter of Zeus." He spit out the name of the king of the gods, piling every pain he had suffered for the last ten thousand years into those four letters. "What can I do for you? My powers are limited, and I am kind of shackled to my job here." He laughed darkly at his own joke.

"All I seek is information."

"Ah, the power of knowledge. If you wanted to know things, why not go to an oracle? They can tell the future, you know. The only thing I know is the open sky. The sky with the eagle coming toward me, and the sky with the eagle going away from me. Oh, and pain, I know a lot about pain."

"I seek knowledge of things that only you know."

"As I told you, I don't know much. Besides, giving knowledge is what got me here in the first place. For a daughter of Zeus, you don't seem to know your history very well."

"You know something that no one else knows. You know of the time before."

"There was no time before this." he said, grinding his teeth and spitting the words out.

She waited until the fire in his eyes was gone before she continued.

"Once, long ago, you escaped to the human world and gave them a gift. You are the only one who has ever done this." She rushed it out so the he would not have time to cut her off. But he did not answer. He didn't even look at her.

"You gave the humans the gift of fire, ten thousand years

ago. Now the humans have turned their backs on us, and we are fading away. Many of the spirits have simply disappeared."

Still he did not respond.

Remembering the beautiful tree at the top of the cliff, she added, "Even most of the nymphs have gone silent." He looked at her then, a tear in his eye.

"There was no time before this," he whispered.

"There was, and you remember it."

"No, I don't. I won't," he insisted, but his words came weakly.

"Prometheus, please. I beg you. I need to know how you did it. I need to know."

"Why? So that you can spend the rest of your life like me? You want this? Look at me. Look at my wrists. Look at my face. Look at the scars, and the places that won't heal."

For the first time, she looked closely at him in the moonlight, and not for the first time, wondered what would happen to her if she failed.

Where the chains met his wrists, there were no shackles. Instead, the chains connected right to the bones in his arm. Or were those odd bumps in his wrists shackles that had simply been there so long that they had become a part of him? His body was covered with scars that she could only assume were from where the great raptor had attacked him when it was not sated by its daily meal of his regrowing liver. His ankles looked much the same as his wrists, but his toes had been torn off; she could only assume by the great bird.

"Is this what you want for the rest of forever?" he barely whispered over the noise of the wind.

"No," she admitted.

"Then just go." He turned his head away from her.

"But I am willing to face it, to help our people." He turned around in surprise and stared at her. She could not read what was behind those eyes, but there was great pain on his face.

"No," he said finally. "No, I will not condemn you to my fate."

"But I am willing."

"No, you are young. You do not know what you are saying."

"Prometheus, we are dying. And I would rather die here on the side of the cliff knowing I had tried than to just fade away knowing I had not."

He was silent a long time after that. So long that her arms began to burn from the strain of hanging on the side of the cliff. She would not die if she fell, but there would be pain and many, many years of healing. She had just about decided to climb back up when he spoke again.

"I didn't do it."

"What?"

"I didn't escape to deliver fire to the humans." The tears were streaming down his face now.

"Of course, you did!"

"No!" he shouted. "No, I didn't." He shifted his weight so that she could see the hole in his side where the great bird tore at him every day. "I didn't take fire to them. I could not, just as you can't now."

"But, then, you have hung here for eons for something you didn't do."

"Please," he said sardonically, "I gave them fire. Of course I did. But I didn't leave the mountain, just like you can't. Like all gifts from the gods, they have to either appear to the humans in such a way that they can see us in the gift, or...." He trailed off again.

"Or?"

"Or they have to be let in to get it."

"Let in? But humans cannot come to Mount Olympus any more than we can go to them."

"They did once. I let them in."

The realization dawned on her then. Although fire was an incredible gift, the idea of humans being on the mountain was probably more than the gods, more than her father, could stand.

"You let them in," she repeated.

"Yes, not very far, but I let them in far enough to come to my campsite. I left a fire burning and let them steal from it. It took years for me to coax a human up that far, and at great risk. If Zeus found out that I had made a way in for them... well in the end he did find out, and you know the rest of the story." He gestured at his prison. His face twisted then, and he cried openly.

She tried to move closer to him to comfort the ancient titan, but he pulled away.

"No!" he croaked. "No, I will not be reminded of what comfort is. It has taken me ten thousand years to forget." She waited until he stopped crying.

"Will you tell me how?"

He didn't answer for a long time, and in the end, he just let his head fall forward in a movement that could have simply been resignation, but she took it as a yes.

"How?"

"Will you come back tomorrow?"

"What?"

"Will you come back tomorrow if I do tell you?"

"If you like."

"I have been so lonely. The nymph in the tree above stopped coming a thousand years ago. Will you talk to her for me?"

She thought back to the beautiful, but silent, tree near the cliff's edge. She wondered how many years it had taken the great titan to convince the nymph to climb down here to visit him. But that explained the hand and footholds.

"I had almost forgotten about her, too, until I heard you tonight."

"Yes, I will come back. But she isn't...." And the pain returned to his face and he looked away again.

"It might be better if you didn't," he said. "I might not have a thousand years to forget you too."

Modern Day

"I've found it!" Larry shouted, standing up in his cubicle. "I found Mount Olympus."

"So? Why not Atlantis, Larry? Sue said, not bothering to get up. "Hundreds of thousands of people have found Mount

Olympus, most notably the Greeks. It's an actual mountain in Greece you know?"

"What?" Rob said. He stood up to look over the wall.

"Mount Olympus! You know, the home of the gods. Come see," he said, ignoring Sue and beckoning Rob over.

Rob hesitated; going over into Larry's cubicle was a bit like stepping into a fantasy world, and more often than not, it wasn't one Rob really wanted to visit. Larry's normal variety of fantasy was not something he enjoyed, but Greek myths were a passion they both shared.

"Come on, it will only take a sec," he said when he saw Rob's hesitation. "It's here on the map."

"All right, I'll bite," Rob said, entering Larry's cubicle. As usual, it was a dizzying array of posters, drawings, and fantasy character figures. They were everywhere: on the desk, on top of his test systems, on the keyboard tray, even on the phone and his monitors.

"Look." Larry pointed to the center of the display on the left. "Here,"

"It looks like a bunch of mountains."

"Right. Let me zoom out a bit so you can get an idea of where they are." He grabbed the mouse and scrolled out so that they could see the whole land mass. It was Greece, of course. Then he zoomed back in.

"Here." He circled a spot on the map with his finger. "Do you see that?"

"It's a mountain, just like all the rest around it." Rob liked Larry. He was a good guy, and he was a brilliant developer, but he was beginning to regret this trip to Larry-land.

"Right. We are looking at the official topographical map. Now if I switch to satellite view..." He clicked and the image changed.

"What's the joke? We're still looking at the same peak."

"Yeah, but look closer. Do you see that shadow?"

"Yes."

"Look at the peaks around it. Do any of them look like that? In fact, have you ever seen a peak that looked that perfect except in drawings?"

Rob looked at the image and Larry was right. There was nothing around that looked like the shadow and it did look particularly perfect.

"Now watch this." He changed the angle of the view so that it was about forty-five degrees from the ground. "Look, look, do you see it?"

"My God!" On the screen, all the other mountains appeared flat, as in most two-dimensional pictures, but the shadow stood up straight; an almost perfect cone. "Wow! That is really cool. I wonder what it is? It has got to be some kind of software glitch."

"No, it's not. I tried it on this other program too. See?" He switched applications and there it was again. "The last one uses flyover views from aircraft. This one uses satellite photos."

"Right. Well, maybe it is one of the other peaks that just looks distorted," Rob said, sitting back down in his own cubicle.

"Yeah, maybe." Larry didn't say anything for a long time.

"I was right!" Larry said right after coming back from lunch with a mailing tube. "I was right, I was right! See, come look at this, Rob!"

Despite the need to get the systems out, Rob was more than a little interested and he really needed a break after the morning he'd had. Sue and Mike both gave him sidelong glances, and Dave, their boss, gave him a look that told him that he would be working overtime if those databases were not up and running.

"What, Larry?"

"Look!" he said, pointing. On his desk were a dozen or so maps of different types and one huge blowup of a satellite image. "I had a friend of mine at NASA get this for me. I owe him about three cases of booze, but it will be worth it."

"What is it?"

"Come on," he insisted, pointing at the image.

Rob looked closer. It was a picture of the same spot Larry

had shown him earlier. The lighting was different, but the shadow still stood exactly as it did before.

"Wow, that is really cool. What do you think it is?"

"Damn it, Rob, don't you believe me? It is Mount Olympus. You know, the home of the gods."

"Larry, that is not possible. It's a myth."

"All myths have their roots in some fact. You, of all people, should know that. In ancient times, no mortal could find it unless the gods wanted you to. I think this is one of those things."

"But why would it show up like this?" Rob said gesturing to the pictures.

"Because you can't hide from photography. The eye you can fool, but not film. And," he said, smiling a little, "I think that maybe they want to be found or at least one of them does."

Rob sat back in the extra chair in Larry's cubicle.

"I have been digging up everything I can on this in the last couple of weeks, and not just on the Internet. I have done some serious bookwork. I have found some really great stuff."

"What about the rollout schedule? Have you been doing the development for that? I am a huge fan of Greek mythology too, but...."

"Forget about that, this is huge. What if we could find our way into the home of the gods? Think of the things we could ask them."

"Larry, we're going live with the first site in less than two weeks."

"Is that all you can think about? Look at this." Larry picked up a book about the stealing of fire from the gods. "This talks about how it only happened because Prometheus, one of the titans who wanted to tweak the nose of Zeus, wanted it to. Think about what it could mean."

"But...."

"But nothing. This is huge."

"Larry, what do you think you are going to find? Besides, Prometheus ended up chained to a cliff getting his liver eaten every day by a giant eagle or something. What do you think you are going to prove?"

"I don't know what I'll find, but I'm going to find something. Right now, I've got to go talk to Dave about some time off." With that, he got up and walked out of his cubicle and headed toward Dave's office.

"Larry, he is never going to give you time off now!" But Larry waved him off and walked right into Dave's office.

They had a short argument that Rob could only guess at, but in the end, Larry threw up his hands, came back to his desk, and spent the next hour or so packing everything up.

"Larry, what are you doing?"

"I quit! Can you believe it? They would not give me the time off when I have found something this big. Dave said something about after the rollout. But what if this thing disappears? What if this is a limited-time offer? What if it is only one god that wants to be found, like I think it might be, and the others find out about it and close the door? We can't wait. We have to get over there now and check this thing out."

"Wait a minute, Larry. I can't go. I have a job to do. We both do. We are grown men; we can't just go running off on a wild goose chase."

"You too? Damn narrow-minded people, can't even see past the ends of your noses. You sound just like the rest of them!" Larry pushed past Rob and walked out.

Later That Afternoon

"Rob?" Rob looked up to see Dave standing at his desk. "I hate to have to do this to you, but it is going to be hard on all of us. Larry quit this morning, as I'm sure you know, so we are going to have to divvy up his rollout responsibilities." Dave always had this way of whining that made Rob's skin want to crawl. It was always worse when he wanted to give bad news. It was as if he picked the most annoying voice to deliver the most annoying news.

"Dave, what did he say?"

"Something about finding Mount Olympus or some

nonsense, and that he needed time off. He was probably lost in one of his video games again. I told him sometime after the rollout was completed, but he insisted that it had to be today. When I told him that was not possible, he quit. Just like that. So, like I said, I am going to need you to do some overtime." There was that voice again.

Modern Day Two weeks later 2:30 AM

Rob woke to the sound of the phone ringing and it made his head hurt.

"Rob, Rob! Wake up, man."

He rolled over to check the clock, and winced as the receiver pressed against his ear.

"Larry?"

"Rob, I've found it! You've got to come see this. It's here."

"Larry, what are you talking about? Do you know what I have been through the last two weeks since you left?"

"Rob, screw all of that. Listen to me. This is huge. I've found it! The entrance to Mount Olympus. I bought you a plane ticket. I need someone here to help me document this. You're the only person I know who would appreciate this. Besides, you are the most detailed person I know. You have to come here. I mean, it is nothing like I expected. It is more than I ever imagined!"

"Larry, hang on a second. What? There is no way. What about work? What about Unitide? What about the rollout?" He was still half-asleep and having a hard time understanding what Larry was talking about.

"Rob, I promise that you will not regret this. Listen, the ticket will be delivered to you first thing in the morning. I have to go." The line went dead.

Rob lay in bed for a long time, not able to get back to sleep. Half of him was cursing Larry for waking him up; half of him was dying to see what Larry had found. Rob had to admit, even with everything he'd been through in the last few weeks, he was interested. He had been since the first day Larry had shown him the photos. He didn't quite know if he should believe Larry, but it was certainly interesting. Besides, although he was a bit odd with all the fantasy things, Larry was not one to really make something like this up. He always did his homework.

For a long time after Rob hung up the phone, he couldn't decide what to do. In the end, practicality won out. If this ticket did show up in the morning, he'd just throw it away and go on like the phone call had never happened. Larry would have to find someone else.

The Next Morning

"Rob, is that your fifth cup of coffee?"

"Yes, Sue, it is."

"Going kind of heavy, aren't you?"

"I didn't sleep well last night."

"But it's not even nine in the morning."

"I have been here since five, Sue." Rob was beyond aggravated with this line of questioning, and made his way to his desk trying not to hear her last comment. She was the kind of person that always had to get the last word in. He had no more than sat down at his desk when his phone rang.

The caller ID showed an inside line, which was both good and bad. It meant that the customer was not having a problem with their newly rolled out system, but it could very well be Dave with a complaint that the customer had.

"This is Rob."

"Rob, this is Mary. You have mail and it is marked urgent."

"Thanks, Mary. I'll be up in a little bit to get it."

"It needs a signature, and it is not marked with Unitide's name. You know the policy about not signing for personal things."

"Yes, yes, I know," Rob said with as much annoyance in his voice as possible. "I will be right up." He hung up the phone and headed for the front desk.

"Not going for more coffee already, are you? You are going to give yourself an ulcer, you know." Sue was at it again, but Rob ignored her.

When Rob got to the front desk, Dave was standing there and he didn't look happy. Apparently Mary had called Dave right after she got off the phone with him. Or maybe right before. One look at the delivery guy, and Rob decided it must have been before. Mary and Dave looked like a firing squad.

"Thank you," Rob said, taking the envelope from the delivery guy and checking that it was addressed to him and not Unitide.

"Just sign here."

"Thank you," Rob said, handing the clipboard back to him. The delivery guy headed for the door without even verifying that Rob had signed on the right line.

"Rob," Dave started as soon as the delivery guy was out the door, and he was using that voice again. "You know the policy about getting personal mail delivered to the office."

"Yes, I do," Rob said turning around. Suddenly he felt like a little kid who got caught stealing a cookie.

"What is this all about? Who is it from?"

He hadn't looked, but he knew it was from Larry.

"Rob? Who is it from?" Now Dave was getting on his nerves too.

"What difference does that make?"

"You are not supposed to be getting mail at the office. It is a distraction. Hand it over and it will be on my desk when you are ready to go home."

"You're kidding, right?"

"Come on, hand it over."

"Like hell."

"You had it delivered here, it is company property."

"Go to hell, Dave," Rob said as he walked back to his desk.

"Rob!" Dave whined as Rob walked away.

Who did Dave think he was? Wasn't it illegal for him to take his mail? Rob decided he'd have to look it up when he got back to his desk.

"Rob, we need to talk about this." Dave must have taken the other way around because now Dave was standing at the entrance to Rob's cubicle.

"What is the deal, Dave? Why all the fuss over a letter?"

"It's from Larry, isn't it?"

"What's the difference?"

"Do you know why the policy is what it is?"

"You know, I never really understood that. You think that grown men and women are going to be distracted by getting mail? We are not three-year-olds, Dave."

"It is what it is. You can have your opinion, but there is more than that. We think Larry could be a security risk since he knew our rollout schedule before he left."

"Bull! Larry never cared about what we were doing here. He was here for the paycheck and you know it!"

"He knew the schedule."

"What did he tell you before he left?" Rob asked.

"Give me the letter, Rob. You can have it back after work."

"I am not a three-year-old," Rob said, raising his voice a bit so that everyone else could hear. "This is total bull. You have no right to take my mail wherever I get it delivered. I have given ten years of loyal service to this company, and you want to treat me like I am a child. Fine! You want the letter, take it." Rob held it above his head, waving it slightly. Dave reached for it, but came about six inches short. Rob smiled at him and walked past him into his cubicle, keeping the letter above his head. He picked up his jacket and keys with his free hand and pushed past him again.

"Where are you going?"

"Same place Larry did. I quit!"

"You can't!"

"Watch me."

A few minutes later, Rob sat with his head on the steering wheel, heart pounding and hands shaking.

"What am I going to do now?" he said to no one. First things first, he needed to go home to get his resume up to date. Then he remembered the letter still sitting on the seat next to him. He felt like it was calling to him, tempting him to open it. He hadn't even wanted the damn letter and now he had quit his job over it.

"What had I been thinking? I wonder if it is too late to go back in." Still, the letter was calling him. He reached over and opened it. Inside was a set of plane tickets, a thousand dollars in cash, and a note.

Rob,

The tickets are for a 2:30 flight so you will have to hurry once you get this. Don't worry about packing. If you need any clothes or anything you can use the money in the envelope. I will pick you up at the Athens Airport.

Larry

"Now what?" He had Larry's money. He was glad that he hadn't run the entire letter through the shredder or given it to Dave. "But now what?"

Greece, Two days later

That morning, Rob found Larry standing in their hotel room, his towel still wrapped around him, a set of maps in one hand and a slice of bread and lox in the other. Larry didn't notice him for a few moments.

"How can you eat that stuff?" Rob said finally, making his way to the coffee pot.

"Oh, good morning, Rob. Sleep okay?"

"Yeah. Where are we? It was pretty late last night when we got in."

"We are in the Olympic National Park, south of Mount Olympus. Here, let me show you." He carried the map to the table with the coffee pot. "Here is Mount Olympus. It's about 2,917 meters tall. Now, here is the GPS unit I bought. See, it has the ability to save previous locations so you can find your way back. I know that it is accurate to about one hundred feet. See, the latitude, longitude, and elevation of this hotel is here, and this is what the GPS shows."

"It only appears to be off by about twelve feet."

"That would be because we're one floor up," Larry said with a smile. "Last week, I climbed up to the highest point on the map, here." He pointed first to the map and then to the GPS. The numbers all matched. "Then using this enlargement of a satellite photo, I found this trail right here." He said pointing to a thin white line on the photo.

"Okay, I see it."

"I followed that path for about ten minutes, and it was pretty steep. Since this is a picture and not exactly the same scale as the map, although it is close, I would guess that I stopped about here and took a GPS reading."

"3,024 meters."

"You know what that means, don't you?"

"Yeah, it means that map is out of date, or wrong or something."

"No. It means that I found the home of the gods!"

"Larry!"

"Rob, listen to me. As soon as I found the trail, everything around me seemed to be shrouded in mist. At first, I didn't really notice it, but the further I went the denser it became."

"You were high enough up that you could have been in a cloud."

"I thought so too, but then when I turned around, I had a really hard time going back down the path. There were even parts I felt like I was going up again, and I can promise you that when I was going up, there were no downhill parts. It was like I kept getting turned around, but the GPS unit said I was going the right way. And here is the kicker: as soon as I was back down at 2,917 meters, no mist, no cloud, nothing."

Could it really be possible that Larry had found what he was looking for? That he had found the fantasy world he had been trying to find all of his life?

"So?" Larry said.

"So, what?"

"Do you believe me?"

"Larry, I'm here. You've given me some pretty hard evidence, but I want to see it for myself before I totally agree." I could not believe the words that were coming out of my mouth.

"Good. It is a two-day hike to the top. You will be glad of all those times I dragged you to the gym with me."

Two Days Later, Mid afternoon

"The path was just over here," Larry said as Rob trailed behind him a few feet. They had reached the peak only a few minutes before.

"Hang on a second, Larry." Rob sat on a nearby rock and

caught his breath. "Larry, I had a thought. What if we get up in the mist like you did and we can't find our way out?"

"That is why we have the extra supplies. They should last us a few days, at least, and longer if we get really lost. But I don't think we will get that lost. We have the GPS unit, and can just keep following it until it eventually leads us out."

"Eventually? That is not very comforting."

"Everything will be fine. You'll see, Rob. Ah, here it is!" He pointed to a little worn spot in the rock. "This is it, just like I told you! Now we just follow this a little ways and we are in. Ready?"

"Larry, I want to make sure that we don't get separated or one of us doesn't fall off some cliff or something. We have about a thousand feet of rope between us. Let's tie the line to our harnesses."

"Wow, how very low-tech of you, Rob, but I'm game."

Rob hooked the rope to each of their harnesses and they started up the path. Within seconds, they were enveloped in a fog so thick, they could hardly see each other.

"Rob, this is about where it happened last time. Go back and see if it feels like you are going up."

Rob picked his way along the path, and, as Larry had said, at points the path seemed to go up and down, even though when they had come in, it was most certainly all uphill. When he finally made his way back down to the base, the fog had indeed cleared. He followed the rope back up to where he'd left Larry.

"Rob? Is that you?" Rob heard Larry's voice just a few feet in front of him.

"Yes."

"Did you hear that?"

"What? You calling to me?"

"No, before that."

"I didn't hear anything. What was it?"

"I thought I heard someone talking."

"No, I didn't hear anything." When Rob was close enough to see him, they stood still and listened for some time, but didn't hear anything.

"You know something weird?" Larry said, breaking the long silence. "When you were walking away, you went down the path, but there were times that I watched the rope, go way up like you were going uphill. Just like I told you."

"Yeah, it was very odd." Rob was starting to feel more than a little nervous. "Let's keep going."

"Right," Larry said, taking the coil of rope from Rob and heading up the path, but he could not hide the slight quiver in his voice. Whether it was from excitement or nervousness, Rob couldn't tell.

"You look a little wiped out," Larry said after a while. "Why don't you take a break and I will scout ahead a bit?"

"Thanks," Rob said. He watched Larry pick his way further up the path, spooling the line out. In truth, he was more than a little tired. He sat down on a nearby rock and waited.

"You finally came," a voice from the mist said.

"Larry?" He didn't answer. Rob pulled gently on the rope and could feel Larry moving away.

"It has been so long," the voice said. It was soft and sweet and definitely not Larry's. Then Rob heard something moving nearby. It sounded like a big animal, but it was coming from a different direction than the voice.

"Who's there?" Rob said, no longer able to hide the fear in his own voice. There was no answer. He yelled for Larry again.

"Coming," Larry said from only a few feet off. "What is it?"

"Larry, the voice you heard before?"

"Yeah?"

"Tell me you heard it again."

"No."

"Larry, there is someone up here with us. And I think they might have brought something with them."

"What do you mean?"

"Like an animal or something, but whatever it was, it sounds huge." They stood and listened again for a few minutes, but again heard nothing.

"Come on, let's keep going," Larry said, a little more

calmly than Rob felt.

"Larry, I am not afraid to admit I am more than a little freaked out."

"Come on, it'll be all right."

"You have nothing to fear," the voice said again.

"I heard that," Larry said.

"Me too." They looked around but could see nothing in the mist.

"Let's keep moving," Larry said. Rob handed the coil of rope to him and they walked on, the voice urging them on now and again.

"Larry, I think we should go back. I mean, we have no idea who or what this is. Didn't they have a lot of sprites and things that liked to play tricks on mortals? They could be leading us to some cliff. We can't see anything in this pea soup."

"Don't go back," the voice said. "You are too far now."

"Rob?"

"What?"

"Did you see that?"

"No, what?"

"I'm not sure, but it was a huge shape." They watched the swirling mist for a few minutes but saw nothing more.

"I am going back," Rob said after a few moments.

"No!" came the voice, more insistent this time. "You will not be able to return."

"You mean we can't leave?" No answer, but now Rob saw something moving in the mist.

"You have come so far," the voice said, sounding as though it was weeping. "Please don't go back."

"Who are you?" Rob asked, but there was no reply.

Rob turned around to go back and bumped into something. It was softer than rock, but just as solid. He backed away and felt something brush against him.

Whatever it was, it was moving around him to prevent him from going either forward or back. Rob fought to keep calm and tried to see through the fog, but could see nothing more than a large vague shape and feel the occasional brush of what felt like hair against his skin.

After what seemed like an eternity, the voice spoke again. "You cannot return, we need you." This time it had more firmness than before, but it was still soft.

"What do you mean?" There was a long silence. Then a figure stepped out of the mist. She was the most classically beautiful woman Rob had ever seen.

"We need your help."

"We?" Larry said. "How could gods need our help?"

"Do not be foolish, mortal. You know something of us or you would not have found the path I made for you," the woman said. "There are certain tasks that only a mortal can do."

"Larry, I don't like this. I know my Greek history too. This usually does not end well for the mortals, who – I feel it my job to remind you – are us." There was a snort from the beast behind him, reminding them both just how right Rob was.

"You could leave," the woman said, "and miss the opportunity to redeem the human race like the heroes of the past. I have been watching you. You have become a soft, pasty people. As if you were made of clay instead of stone like your ancestors."

"Who are you?" Rob asked.

"I am Nikoleta, the last daughter of Zeus and Hera."

"See, Rob, I told you. We have made it."

"You were right, Larry. But she is not telling us what she wants of us."

"Yes, you have made it to Mount Olympus, and the task I have for you is to help me free my uncle. He has been imprisoned for most of human history for a transgression that he need no longer be punished for. Will you help me? Will you be the heroes that you can be, or will you be the cowardly race our history has shown us you have become?"

"Who is your uncle?"

"Follow me," she said.

They followed her through the mists for what felt like

hours. The ground was level now, but the mists never parted.

"How do you know where you are going in this mist?" Larry asked.'

"He said you might not be able to see clearly. I am sorry. For us, there are no mists. That is the price you pay for being mortal in a place of immortals. We have arrived."

"Where are we?"

"These are the cliffs where my uncle is being held. Only a mortal can free him."

"Your uncle is Prometheus?" Larry asked, stepping closer to the cliffs and looking down.

"You know your history. At least you have not forgotten that much."

"I also know that only Hercules' blade was strong enough to break the chains. And that Hercules once freed him from this prison," Larry said.

"Why is he back here?" Rob asked.

"I am impressed, mortals." She gestured with her hand and a huge beast stepped out of the mists holding a bag. It looked something like a man, only many times bigger and covered in fur. There were hooves where its feet should be. Nicoleta took the bag from the creature and pulled out a short sword. "My brother's sword." She held it out to Larry. "As to why he is here again, my father is to blame. He could not stand the idea that Prometheus had given such a great gift to the humans. Then Zeus was angry that the humans thought they were so much better than us that they could forget about us. So he locked my uncle back up."

"I have been studying you my whole life," Larry said when finally he tore his eyes off the huge beast. She blushed slightly at this. "Well, not you in particular. Your family. I didn't even know about you until just now, but if I had, believe me, I would have studied you too."

"What my friend is saying is, why are we freeing Prometheus, and what is that?"

"He is the one who told me how to get you here. It was part of the deal. He tells me how to get mortals here, and the mortals free him before helping me. And that is my brute. At one time they were Minotaur, but they have mixed with regular beasts and much of their human qualities are gone."

"Larry, we need to talk about this. I mean, the gods I read about were not very forgiving. Even if we are helping one or two of them out, we could be crossing several others. This could be a very bad idea."

"Rob, come on. This is a chance to do a heroic deed. We need to do this. Besides, I am pretty sure she risked her life to bring us here."

She nodded. "I have risked a great deal to bring you here. If my father were to find out...."

"You see what I mean, Larry? She did risk a lot to bring us here, but her father tends to have a heavy hand when it comes to dealing with people who have gone against him."

"This will be easy. I lower you down - one swipe should break each of the chains - and then you come back up and we can get out of here. Maybe Nikoleta can come with us and answer some questions. Can you imagine, Rob? She likely knows the answers to many of the mysteries of human history."

"But what else is it she wants us to do?"

"We must free Prometheus. Nothing else."

Rob looked skeptically at them both one more time, and took the sword from her.

The humans had proved capable, just as she had known that anyone who could find their way into Olympus must be. She was beginning to believe that some of what the other gods had told her about humans being stupid and having lost their heroic spirit was wrong.

Within five minutes, the one called Larry had lowered his friend over the side and they worked to free Prometheus.

"Why do you keep touching that tree?" Larry asked, startling her out of her thoughts.

"It was a friend of Prometheus."

"Was?"

"She faded," Nikoleta said, walking from the tree to look

over the cliff's edge.

Rob had neared Prometheus and was beginning to work at the chains that held the titan in place. Rob cut the last of the chains and swung away from the titan. The giant old god swung around, almost knocking Rob from the side of the cliff as he grappled his way to the top. As he cleared the edge, he nearly knocked Larry and Nikoleta to the ground trying to reach the tree. When he got to it, he fell to his knees and wept.

"What is going on?" Rob asked when he finally got to the top himself.

"She was the only one who gave him comfort in the last ten thousand years. She would come down and see him. She had been with him since the beginning."

"Her?"

"A tree nymph." Larry replied.

"What happened to her?"

"She faded." Prometheus stood. "Nikoleta, we should go and get these two back to the doorway before your father finds out they are here."

As if on cue, the sky split with a great flash of lightning.

"You need to go, girl."

"Where would I go?"

"Away. Far away."

"But what about them?"

I will do what I can for them, but your father is not going to take kindly to their being here."

"But Prometheus...."

"No, daughter of Zeus, it is time for you to leave. I will do what I can for them, but you must leave before your father finds you here."

When she had gone, Prometheus sat down next to his beloved tree and wept.

"I thought you were going to help us?" Rob said.

"There is no help for any of us, but I could not take her hope away."

"Should we fight?" Larry asked drawing the sword of Hercules.

"You are going to fight the gods?"

Four brutes stepped from the mists, followed by several smaller creatures.

"What will happen to us?"

"If you are lucky, the brutes will throw you from the cliff to your death."

"And if we are not lucky?" Rob asked.

"They will chain you to the side of the mountain beside me, and the eagle will have a great feast of three livers tomorrow morning and every morning hence."

"This is not how I pictured it ending up for us, Larry." Rob said as the last of the chains was attached to the rock.

"Me neither, my friend. Me neither."

Tunnel in the Sky

by Michell Plested

Scoutmaster Charlemagne stood watching his troop assemble. After more than two years planning, fundraising, and training, they were finally going to do it. They were finally going to get their chance to go off-planet. This was more than a once-in-a-lifetime chance. Most citizens would never have an opportunity to go off-world. Not that many wanted to.

Charlemagne had been off-world before, of course. That was part of his regular job; a thirty-year veteran Marine sergeant, the scouts were his chance to relax and give something back to the next generation.

Around them, technicians prepared the gate for the transport. All the troop's equipment for the two-week trip was in the packs they carried on their backs. Stoves, knives, food, clothing, and shelter. If they didn't bring it and carry it with them, they would have to do without.

For their part, the scouts were almost buzzing with excitement. Most hadn't even been to one of the handful of nature preserves left on Earth. To suddenly leave the comfort of civilization to travel to an untamed wilderness planet, even one owned by the World Scouting Organization, was too fantastic to comprehend.

And now, the departure day was finally here. And to make it sadder for those not coming, the fundraising had been a spectacular success. The troop had managed to raise enough money to completely pay their own way. Those who had left the troop would never get another chance to see nature unsullied by the hand of man.

One of the technicians stepped up to Charlemagne. "I'm going to need to see your identification, sir. Yours and all your troop before we can commence the pre-transport sequence."

"Certainly," Charlemagne answered, pulling his identification tags from under his camo.

The man scanned the tags and nodded toward the scouts. "Them next."

"Troop!" Charlemagne used his parade voice to cut through the noise of the area and the troop's chatter. The scouts stiffened at the sound and went silent facing their troop master. "Troop, pull out your identification tags so we can get this little shindig underway."

The technician went to each youth, scanning their tags one at a time. When he was done, he nodded at Charlemagne. "Everything is in order. We will start spinning up the transport generators. Should only be another thirty minutes or so."

"Thank you," Charlemagne responded. He began walking among the troop. "Do you all have your gear ready to go?"

Several of the youth gave Charlemagne the thumbs up. A couple opened their packs to double-check their gear.

"Remember folks, we will be off-planet for two weeks. There are no commissaries or grocery stores on Garden. World Scouting has purposely left the planet as pristine as possible. That means no latrines, no power, and no pollution. It also means there will be wild animals, some of which are predators, that won't think twice about trying to snack on any one of us. Is that understood?"

"Yes, Troop Master Charlemagne," the group shouted in

unison.

"Very good. Now, I want Kailee to take the lead through the transport when it's ready. The rest of you will follow her and I will bring up the rear. Each of you is to wear your pack and all other gear. That will prevent anything from being lost in transport. I will also carry most of the rations, since they weigh the most. That being said, each of you should have a day's worth of food in your kit. Any questions?"

"No, Troop Master Charlemagne," the troop shouted again.

"Excellent! Now, this will be your last time to use civilized facilities for some time so I suggest you hit them while you can." Charlemagne grinned as the entire troop practically ran toward the transport center's bathroom facilities.

"Sir, we are about a minute from transport. Is your troop ready?" the technician asked.

Charlemagne looked at his troop. Most of them had been with him from the time they had first entered scouting. He couldn't think of a finer group of young people. "We are ready," he replied, looking them over again. Better get them prepared. "Kailee!"

"Yes, Troop Master Charlemagne?"

"When you go through the portal, have your combat knife ready. There's really no telling what will be waiting for us on the other side."

The girl flipped her wrist and a long serrated blade was suddenly in her hand. "Will do, Troop Master."

Charlemagne grinned. That was one girl who knew how to take care of herself. He still remembered the incident all those months ago. It seemed a few recalcitrant youth had decided to have some sport with Kailee, thinking her easy prey. When she was done with them, only one of the attackers would never have a chance to procreate again. A Peace Forcer had come by to try and recruit the girl even though she was still a minor.

The hum of spinning-up generators filled the air.

"Okay, troop. Line up like we practiced. Let's show these civilians what real scouts look like."

The troop wasted no time getting into their transport lineup. At that moment, Charlemagne couldn't have been prouder.

The technician looked down on the troop from a raised platform and spoke into a megaphone. "Okay, scouts. I'm about to begin my countdown. I will count from ten to one. When I say one, you will see a vortex form in the transport cradle. Waste no time. Run into the vortex immediately. Do you understand?"

Kailee spoke for the group. "We understand, sir. Run into the vortex when you say one." Her voice vibrated with command and confidence.

"Um, er, yes...indeed," the technician said. He checked his tablet and began the countdown. "Ten, nine, eight..."

When he said one, the vortex formed, barely visible. Kailee wasted no time and jogged directly into it. Each member of the troop ran to follow her. One by one, they disappeared into the swirling tunnel of dark energy.

Charlemagne was almost to the vortex when the humming of the generators started to change to a squeal. "Pick it up, troop. Sounds like the transport might be about to shut down."

The troop picked up the pace, sprinting into the energy. While the noise around them rose to an almost painful level, Charlemagne was just about to step into the vortex when he was hit by a wall of sound.

"Sir, are you all right?"

Charlemagne opened his eyes to see the blurry image of someone leaning over him. "Where am I?"

"Sir, you are in the transport facility infirmary. An ambulance has been called and should be here shortly."

"Is everyone okay? How is my troop?" Charlemagne asked, struggling to sit up in the bed.

"Now you just relax, sir. You have suffered some trauma

and we need you to remain calm." The features of the blurry figure slowly gained focus until Charlemagne could see the medtech was an older woman.

"Ma'am, you haven't answered my question. Are the members of my troop safe?"

The same technician Charlemagne had dealt with on the transport floor stepped into his visual range. "That's a difficult question to answer, Troop Master. The explosion didn't occur until after your troop was all through the portal. We believe they arrived at Garden safely but, until we have everything restored to full working order, we have no way to confirm it."

"So, what you're saying is, they could be safe or they could be dead?" Charlemagne began struggling to get up again.

"Troop Master, if you don't lie still I'm going to have to sedate you," the medtech said. "As I told you, your troop all made it into the portal. We don't know what happened to cause the explosion and we are not willing to speculate until more investigation has happened.

Charlemagne lay back, carefully taking shallow breaths. His troop, kids who had grown up with him, was in trouble. He could feel it deep in his gut. And he was here, stuck, unable to help them, guarded by a medtech ready to sedate him if he tried to move.

"How soon will you have the transporter back up and functional? I've got to get to them...."

Charlemagne then realized he had all the food and larger pieces of gear. "Oh, my heavens. I've got most of their food. They need me so they don't starve!"

"Troop Master, I know the requirements for troops like yours," the transport technician said. "Your kids have to have a very high level of self-reliance. They can survive on their own until we get the system back up and running."

"When will that be? You still haven't told me how long it will take!" Charlemagne could feel his heart rate increasing. He was starting to feel dizzy. The room was fading away.

"Troop Master? Troop Master! Oh crap, get me a sedative.

This guy is about to either stroke out on us or have a heart attack," the medtech yelled.

The cool bite of a hypo-syringe hit Charlemagne in the neck and he knew no more.

Kailee hit the ground hard coming out of the portal. She automatically ducked into an awkward roll as the backpack threw her off-balance. What the hell had that been? She hadn't ever been in a transport portal before but no one had ever mentioned a twisting sensation.

She got up and moved out of the portal's exit pathway. It wouldn't do to be hit by one of her troop. She took a good look around. If this was Garden, it sure didn't match any of the descriptions she had heard. The trees were all wrong. Charlemagne had thoroughly briefed them on the deciduous trees that forested the region they were going to. These trees weren't like anything he had described. They looked almost... well, they looked like they were wearing robes. That couldn't be right, could it?

And the temperature wasn't as warm as she had heard either. Even through her layers of gear, Kailee felt the cold. She shivered. If the trees were wrong and the weather was wrong, where were they?

Another member of her troop hurtled through the portal. He lay in a heap where he landed. Kailee hurried to his side. It was Kenneth. He hadn't been right behind her. That had been Lianal. Kenneth had been third in line. She checked for a pulse. It was weak, but it was there. She pulled him to the side and made him comfortable. The weirdness just kept coming.

Several seconds later, another body came through. Amyline rolled much like Kailee had and jumped to her feet. The girl saw Kailee and trotted over.

"That was odd," Amyline said. "What happened to Kenneth?"

"Don't know. He was out when he got here. Watch over him while I help the next through."

One by one the rest of the troop arrived, some conscious, some not. All but Lianal. Kailee continued to stand watch.

The portal began to shrink in on itself. Still no Lianal. It was only slightly wider than a man's head when the last member of the troop came out. The sides of the portal sheared off Lianal's shoulders and most of his torso. Lianal hit the ground screaming and writhing like a skinned worm.

Kailee could only watch in horror as her troop mate bled out and stopped moving. The sound of screaming was pounding at her ears. That was when she realized she was the one still screaming.

"Oh my God!" Amyline said, running to Kailee's side. "Is that Lianal?"

Tears ran down Kailee's cheeks. She sniffed and wiped her nose with her sleeve. "Was Lianal. Was. Get a detail together to dig a grave for him, please."

Amyline looked around. "Where's the troop master? Where is Charlemagne?"

Kailee shook her head. "Not here, wherever that is. Now, please, Amyline, let's get a grave dug for Lianal before any animals come."

"I say we go looking for Charlemagne," Rashan said, striking a dramatic pose and looking down at the reclining troop. "He will know what to do."

Kailee sighed. "As I've already said a dozen times, Rashan, looking for Charlemagne is a waste of time. What if he didn't even come through the portal? What if he is somewhere else entirely? And on that topic, we don't even know where here is exactly."

"Obviously, we are on Garden," Rashan said, frustration creeping into his voice.

"But where exactly? I don't see anything like the identifying marks we were given for the drop site," Kailee said. "Rashan, run all the identifying features Charlemagne drilled us on. Does any of this match any those?"

"Maybe not," Rashan said. "And that is exactly my point.

We are not where we should be and Charlemagne is missing. We should scout our position and find the troop master."

"Looking for Charlemagne will do us no good. We need to follow our training."

"And what?" Rashan asked with a sneer. "Set up camp and wait for rescue? Have you forgotten that Charlemagne had most of our food? What do you propose we eat?"

"Rashan, you know very well we all packed trail rations," Amyline said. "Each of us should have enough for several days. I know they taste like crap, but they will keep us alive and healthy."

"Not all of us bothered," Rashan said. "Some of us used the weight allocation to bring other things."

"What?" Kailee said. "What could you possibly have brought that is more important than food?"

"I don't know about Rashan, but I brought a pillow and heavier ground pad," Tean said. The boy was easily the largest of the troop and also easily the least intelligent. He was built much like an old-world bull and was probably close in strength to one. "I wanted to get some shut-eye while we were on Garden. That flimsy junk we were issued barely made any difference at all for me."

"And I brought a small, but extremely lethal gun. It works using compressed air and poisoned darts. I'll be able to hunt and have as much food with that as I want," Rashan said. He pulled the weapon out of a pocket in his pack and flashed it at the group. "Don't any of you get any ideas about stealing this or there will be trouble!"

"None of us will steal your precious gun." Kailee shook her head. "And I cannot believe you would bring a banned device. Charlemagne will have your nuts in a sling over this."

"If he isn't dead," Rashan said. "Even if he still lives, Charlemagne isn't here. I would gladly hand over the gun if he were, but he isn't, so you should be thanking me for bringing it."

"Just put your gun away, Rashan, and get to work, okay?" Kailee said.

"Get to work? Don't you think we should put this to a

vote?" Rashan asked, his voice filled with surprise. "This is all our lives. Poor Lianal never even had a chance. I, for one, don't want to end up like him."

"Vote?" Kailee laughed. "This isn't a democracy, Rashan. Never has been, never will be. Charlemagne put me in charge, so what I say goes."

"I think my gun gives me a vote, Kailee, don't you?" Rashan sneered. "There isn't much you can do if I start calling the shots around here." He thought about what he had just said. "Shots. Ha. That's pretty funny, if I do say so myself."

Kailee snapped her fingers and the remaining members of the troop jumped to their feet.

"Can you stop all of us, Rashan? I know how those little dart pistols work. I know you have to lever pump the pistol to reset the pressure after each shot. You might hit one of us, but then the rest of us will stop you. I promise you, you won't like your punishment. Oh, and just so you know, I have a medical kit with me that contains a general antidote, so, if your poisoned darts aren't anything new, it won't really do much damage anyway."

Rashan looked at his pistol. "Fine! Have it your way. We can set up camp and wait." He put the gun back into his pocket.

"How about being a good boy and just give me that little piece of contraband, hmm?" Kailee asked. "That way I know you are sincerely a team player."

Rashan smiled then. "No. If it's all the same to you, I think I'll just hold onto the gun."

"Have it your way, Rashan. But if I see it again, I will take it away from you," Kailee said.

"Yes, Mother," Rashan said, pitching his voice so it sounded nasally. He moved away from the fire they had burning to a flat area where he turned over his backpack, dumping out the contents. "I assume it's all right if I set up here?"

"Perfectly fine, Rashan. Knock yourself out," Kailee said. She looked at the other youth. "Okay, troop. You've done this many times in practice. Let's get this camp set up, shall we?"

"Yes, Troop Leader," All the voices, except Rashan's, said together in a chorus.

Kailee had to admit the camp looked good. The regulation lightweight tents were all pitched in a neat rectangle. All, that is, except for Rashan's. His was noticeably absent from the pattern. His was pitched up in a tree where he had built himself a small platform.

She shook her head. Whatever he wanted to do was fine as long as he didn't put the entire group at risk. Admittedly, the ground wasn't tactically the best place to be, but until Kailee knew more about the terrain, she wanted to be somewhat close to the gate in case anyone came through it.

Kailee looked up at Rashan's tree tent and giggled. It would certainly be too bad if Rashan decided to go for a night stroll. That would be the first, and last, step he made. In her mind's eye she pictured the arrogant guy falling out of his tree, screaming all the way down.

She would pay good money to see that, and Kailee suspected many of her fellow scouts would too.

"Rashan, I don't suppose you will stand first watch?" Kailee called up to the tree structure.

A stick sailed out of the elevated tent, landing at her feet.

"That's what I thought you would say, Rashan," she said. "Fine, I will take first watch instead. Just to be clear though, you will either contribute to this troop or you're on your own." She walked away from the tree and back to camp without looking back.

Kailee settled into a watch routine. She turned her back to the fire to maintain her night sight. That was one advantage they had. Anything coming into camp would have to contend with the glare of the campfire.

Kailee heard the scrunching of boots on the ground behind her. "Troop Leader?"

"Cristoff? What's going on?" Kailee asked. Cristoff hadn't said much after Lianal came through the gate. As the troop medic, he had seen his share of blood, so that shouldn't have been it.

"Troop Leader...Kailee...do you have any idea where we might be?"

"Where? I assume we are somewhere on Garden," Kailee said. "That was where we were being sent, after all. I don't fully understand the transporters but I do know they need pretty specific coordinates to pinpoint a planet."

Cristoff crouched down beside Kailee. "Protein bar?" he asked, holding out a wrapped rectangle. At Kailee's head shake, he stowed the bar in a vest pocket. "Kailee, I haven't said anything to anyone about this until now, but I think we are on an entirely different planet than Garden."

"And what led you to that?" Kailee asked, watching the darkness for any kind of movement.

"You may not know this, but I'm actually a bit of an amateur astronomer. When I heard we were going to Garden, I read up on the planet's visible stars and constellations for both the northern and southern hemispheres," Cristoff said.

"So?"

"So, the stars above us are not the stars I studied."

Kailee looked up at the sky. A sliver of moon was coming up from the west and a myriad of stars twinkled above in the cold night air.

"I'm sorry, Cristoff, but it's going to take more than your word that the stars are wrong. I'm not an astronomer like you, but I did take a couple courses in school. I'm sure you wouldn't argue that the visible stars change depending on the season and where you are on the planet. It could just be that the stars you studied were for the wrong time and/or place."

"I wish you were right," Cristoff said. "Unfortunately, the stars in Garden's skies are few; Garden is actually near the edge of our Spiral Arm galaxy. Look up in the sky Troop Leader. There are thousands. Maybe even hundreds of thousands."

"And maybe you just got the count wrong. Or maybe you were studying the wrong side of the planet," Kailee said. She knew her words sounded lame, but it was better than admitting they were on a totally different planet.

"Possibly," Cristoff said. "But there is one piece of evidence even you cannot ignore or explain away."

"Oh, what's that?" Kailee asked.

"Garden has no moon, and that," Cristoff pointed at the sliver, "clearly is one. I'm pretty sure I saw another earlier tonight too. Just a tiny one that moved incredibly fast across the sky."

But Kailee wasn't listening. She had just finished searching her own memory of the planet and Cristoff was right. Garden had no moon.

Kailee took the entire night's watch, her mind being too busy to allow her any peace. If they weren't on Garden, where were they? Wherever it was, they definitely were not alone. Kailee had seen several sets of eyes reflect the firelight from the darkness beyond the camp. At least they hadn't done more than stare at the fire.

As the sun rose, Cristoff, looking like he hadn't slept either, came up to Kailee. "Didn't you sleep last night? Why didn't you wake one of us?"

"Couldn't sleep," Kailee said. She was staring up where Rashan had set up his tent. She pointed at it. "Does anything about that look wrong to you?"

Cristoff shaded his eyes and looked where Kailee pointed. "Isn't that where Rashan set up?"

"Yeah, but I don't remember his gear being quite that lumpy or that color," Kailee said. She cupped her hands around her mouth. "Hey, Rashan! Are you going to sleep the day away or are you going to come down here and make yourself useful?"

When Rashan didn't respond, Kailee picked up the stick Rashan had tossed at her the night before. She took aim and threw the stick up at the sleeping figure. The stick sailed true and struck Rashan's tent.

That's when the lump revealed itself to be something else.

A flock of winged reptiles launched themselves off the branch and flew up, their leathery wings pumping the air. They circled the camp a few times before they moved off. Kailee rushed to her pack and pulled out a pair of binoculars and trained them on Rashan's last position. She stood frozen, looking at the tree for almost a minute before she lowered them again.

"What do you see?" Cristoff asked.

Kailee wordlessly handed him the binoculars and waited while he took a look himself. When he finally spoke, Cristoff was looking a little green. They picked him clean."

"At least what we can see," Kailee agreed.

"What's going on?" Amyline asked, joining them.

"See for yourself," Cristoff said, giving the girl the binoculars.

"Amyline looked through the binoculars. What am I supposed to...." Her words stopped as she finally saw Rashan's remains. She ran to a nearby bush where she loudly vomited.

She handed Kailee the binoculars when she came back. "What happened to Rashan?"

Kailee shook her head. "I'm not sure. There were some sort of avian creatures up in there this morning. Maybe they got him, or maybe something else did. Whatever they were, they weren't in any of the books I studied about Garden before we came. And Cristoff pointed out that the stars are all wrong too."

"So, what are we going to do?" Amyline's voice was almost a wail.

"We're going to have a troop meeting," Kailee said. "Could you round up the others and have them come here, please?"

Seven expectant faces looked at Kailee. She was used to being in command of the group. Just not used to making all the decisions. But now they had lost two people. Like it or not, their lives had been in her hands, and the lives of the rest were her responsibility too. Right now, she wasn't sure she wanted it. But she had trained for it and the burden was hers to carry.

"Here is what we know." She kept her voice as strong as possible. "Something went wrong with the transport. We lost Lianal in that accident and Charlemagne may or may not also be gone. We also know we are not on Garden." That caused some comments. Kailee waited a full thirty seconds before she interrupted the group. "We know we are not on Garden because the stars are wrong and because we have already seen evidence of flora and fauna that doesn't match anything we know about Garden."

"So, what are we going to do?" Pedro Rodriguez asked.

"We are going to survive as best we can," Kailee answered. "To start, I need to know who brought weapons."

"I've only got my knife," Ivy Scalings, a petite blonde, said, stepping forward. "And, I know how to make a few things: spears, bow and arrow, and the like."

"That will help, Ivy. Thanks," Kailee said. "Anyone else have anything besides knives? Any projectile or energy weapons?"

"Kailee, we were expecting to be camping, not going to war," one of the boys said. "I would have happily brought those things, but Charlemagne said NO."

Kailee nodded at the boy. "I know, Richard. That didn't stop Rashan from bringing a dart gun with him."

"Didn't do him much good though, did it?" Amyline asked.

"No, it didn't," Kailee said. She didn't add that she felt responsible for his death. If she had just convinced him to stay with the troop, he might still be with them. If he hadn't died, they might still have his weapon to protect them. "But we are on an unknown world. We already know predators are out there. We need to prepare as well as we are able for whatever might be coming."

"And what might that be?" another one of the boys asked. "When the heck are the rescuers going to come get us? Why are you telling us we have to get ready to fight?"

Kailee shook her head and tried to keep her voice steady. What she had to say was hard. "Andrew, we don't even know if rescue is coming. For that to happen, somebody back home has to know where we are. Since we ended up here instead of Garden, I don't know how likely that is. I'm trying to prepare us all in case something nasty comes our way. Okay?"

The boy, Andrew, nodded, his face white. "So what do you want us to do?"

"Thanks, Andrew. Can I put you in charge of inventorying everything we have? Food, clothes, water, tools, and weapons, please?"

At his nod, Kailee continued. "Ivy, can you take a couple volunteers and gather what you need to make any weapons you can? Make sure you all stay out of tall grass and thick trees, just like Charlemagne taught us, okay?"

"You got it, Kailee," Ivy said. "Come on, Pedro. You too, Suzy." Ivy grabbed a pretty redhead by the elbow and guided her and Pedro away from the group.

"Come on, Cristoff," Kailee said. She started walking toward Rashad's tree.

Cristoff started to follow. "Where are we going, Kailee?"

"Rashad had a dart pistol. Knowing there are predators around, I think it's worth the effort to retrieve it along with any other gear he might have. It isn't like he will need it now and I would like to know what killed him."

Cristoff frowned. "Are you sure that's wise?"

"Rashad got up into that tree easily enough. I'm not worried. Besides, it's light out and I'm not asleep. I know something is dangerous so I will be extra careful."

"Whatever you say," Cristoff said. "Just don't take any silly risks, okay?"

Kailee laughed. "That much I can promise you." She grabbed a low branch and lifted her foot to it, beginning the climb.

The branches were close enough together that Kailee was able to scale the tree easily. She quickly made her way up to the branch Rashad had camped on. She could already smell the body's decay as she got closer.

The branch was wide and she was able to walk along it without trouble. As she got closer to Rashad's shredded tent and sleeping bag, she noticed something odd. Branches seemed to be growing out of the top. At first, Kailee thought it was wood that had been knocked off the tree. Upon closer inspection, she could see it was actually right though the body and the bag. And that had happened since the previous day.

It took her a few minutes to find Rashad's backpack. The bag, brightly colored, should have been easy to see. But, like the fast-grown branches through the sleeping bag, the tree's bark had grown over the pack. Only the dark top strap was showing at all.

Kailee pulled her knife and began hacking at the tough bark.

Three sharp whistle blasts pulled her attention from the cutting.

Kailee looked toward the source of the sound. Ivy and Pedro were running as if the hounds of hell were chasing them. She looked past them for Suzy. That's when she saw what looked like a cross between a lion and a wolf running after the pair.

The creature was catching up to them with every stride, its mouth open in a snarl she could not hear. The hounds of hell had nothing on it.

Pedro stumbled and almost fell. That was enough to allow the monster to make up the remaining distance. It leaped on Pedro and in a few brief moments Kailee saw the thing tear Pedro apart.

Her studies on Earth predators didn't prepare her for what happened next. Rather than settle on Pedro's remains for the meal it represented, the creature immediately went back into pursuit mode, chasing after Ivy.

The girl had only stopped long enough to see Pedro was done for before she had started running again. That had opened the gap between her and the animal, but not by enough. Ivy was starting to slow down and the murderous creature seemed, if anything, faster.

Kailee could only watch helplessly as Ivy was run down just like Pedro had been. There was still no sign of Suzy.

Kailee didn't think there ever would be.

Just like with Pedro, the creature was on its feet and running as soon as Ivy was dispatched. This time it was directly toward the camp. The creature was coming for them!

"Everyone, get up in the trees! Hurry!" Kailee screamed to the remaining troop.

"What's going on?" Cristoff called up to her.

"Don't ask questions. Just get everyone up into the trees. I'll explain when you are all safe." Kailee didn't wait to see if they obeyed. She started hacking at the overgrown backpack, hoping to find the weapon Rashad had flashed around the previous night. She could hear the troop shouting at each other in confusion but didn't look back. The attacking monster wasn't far enough away to allow her to waste any precious time.

Her blade bit into the bark over and over tearing out chunks of the wood. A sticky ichorous sap started to flow from the wound in the tree. Slowly the backpack was revealed.

Kailee risked a look over her shoulder. The monster was almost into the camp, still moving fast. She didn't see any of the troop. That was promising. She kept working the backpack out of its cocoon.

"Do you need any help?"

Kailee screamed, almost falling out of the tree in her surprise. She turned to smack Cristoff for scaring her and froze. A massive serpentine creature was poised just behind Cristoff preparing to strike.

Moisture dripped off exposed fangs in the thing's mouth.

"Cristoff, look out," Kailee managed to whisper.

Cristoff, seeing the terror in Kailee's face slowly turned. The creature struck then, taking Cristoff full in the face. Both boy and snake-thing tumbled out of the tree to the ground.

Cristoff didn't move after hitting the ground. Kailee, feeling faint with fear and shock, looked for the rest of the troop, hoping to find them in the trees.

No one.

She looked back down to the ground where the serpent

was swallowing her friend. Cristoff had almost entirely disappeared into its mouth, his body making a large bulge in the creature's body.

A roar turned her attention toward the camp. The lion-wolf was walking toward her tree, looking directly at her.

Kailee frantically finished digging the top of the backpack out and opened the bag. The small gun was inside, right on top.

She silently thanked Rashan for disobeying Charlemagne's rules as she pulled out the compact dart pistol and quickly checked it over. Fully loaded and operational.

The sound of claws on bark pulled her attention away from the gun to the base of the tree. The monster had begun climbing toward her.

There was no time to lose. Kailee pumped up the weapon, flipped the weapon's safety off and fired at the climbing animal. A tiny dart struck the thing in the shoulder. It continued to climb for several seconds more, getting closer to Kailee. Just as she was about to panic, wondering if the poison would work, the creature stiffened and stopped moving. Soundlessly, the lion-wolf fell from the tree onto the bloated body of the serpent.

The force of the fall on the serpent split the creature's belly exposing the still form of Cristoff in its guts. The snake-thing writhed as it died and went still, its head still opening and closing in a grisly display. The lion-wolf lay where it fell, its body twisted.

Kailee sank down into a sitting position, her back against the tree, and started to sob. Something wet struck her hand as cried. She looked down at it just as the next droplet of sap from the tree struck her.

Charlemagne, dressed in full combat gear, stood waiting for the generators to spin up. It had been almost a week since the accident. He had spent most of that time recovering in the medlab. He was glad to see the transporter techs hadn't wasted their time getting the system back online, figuring out what had gone wrong and tracking down his troop.

"Okay, people. Let's get this portal spun up so I can get back to my troop," Charlemagne commanded.

"Yes, sir," one of the techs said, beginning to activate the portal dimensional gear.

Charlemagne looked at the shock troops that waited behind him. "Okay, folks. You know what the tech-heads over there found when they were doing their accident investigation. My little darlings were not transported to Garden like they were supposed to be. Somehow they ended up going to an interdicted world. We don't know what we will find. Only that we need to bring my troop back if possible. Understood?"

"Yes, sergeant," the shock troop corporal said.

The whine of the generators grew and the transport alarms sounded.

"Okay, then. Follow me through as soon as the transport rift is stable," Charlemagne said, turning toward the growing gate. He gave his pulse rifle one last check before he ran toward the now stable transport gate.

The camp, what was left of it, was in a shambles, the bodies of the troop torn apart and rotting in the sun.

Charlemagne stood watching the scene impassively. The time to mourn would come. Now needed a clear head. "Corporal, take some men and find me all of my kids. You have the frequencies of their trackers. I'll do what I can to collect the casualties here."

"Yes, sergeant," the corporal said. He gathered four men and took to the fields searching for the missing troop.

Charlemagne took the remaining men and began the grisly job of gathering remains. He carefully placed each dead member of the troop he found into a separate body bag. The sixth body was sprawled among the rotting corpses of two monsters at the base of a tree.

"Sir, if this is what came after your troop, it's no wonder

they were killed. They couldn't have been prepared for this kind of predator."

Charlemagne shook his head. "Only one of the troop had the right training and we haven't found her yet. The rest, as good as they were, wouldn't have had a chance." He raised his wrist communicator. "Corporal, how many have you found?"

"Sir, we are bringing back three bodies. One was about half a mile from the camp. The other two were within sight of it."

"Only three? We have five here. That means two are missing."

"Sir, my sensors show seven trackers at the camp."

"What?" Charlemagne swore at himself. He had been so busy collecting the bodies he saw, he hadn't bothered to switch the tracking gear on. He quickly flipped the tracker on, noting the three blips close to each other near the gate. Then one off behind the camp and the three at the tree... He swore again. The boy was one. Where were the others?

"Search the area. There are two more here somewhere." He pointed toward the single signal. "I need a team to check for a lone body over there."

The men spread out and searched the area to no avail. Where were the other trackers?

"Sir?" the corporal's voice came from his communicator.

"Go ahead, corporal."

"Sir, I found a shallow grave. Body belongs to a male. And you should check up in the tree. I can see something up on one of the high branches. It looks manmade."

Charlemagne nodded his head at a trooper who dropped his pack to climb the tree. It was only a matter of a minute before he shouted down.

"Sir, there is one body in a sleeping bag up here."

"Man or woman?"

"Not sure, sir. The body is picked pretty clean. I would guess a male by the skeleton."

Any sign of the other?"

"Not up here, sir."

Charlemagne searched his mind. Who was missing? Then

it hit him. "Where the hell is Kailee?"

"Sir, you are going to want to see this," one of the grunts called from near the snake-creature body.

"See what, private? What are you getting at?"

"You need to come and see, sir."

Grumbling, Charlemagne put down his pack and strode over to the man, carefully stepping over the body of the dead scout Cristoff. "What is so important you need me to see it personally?"

The private pointed to the dead snake-creature. "I found the last transmitter, sir."

"Kailee's? Where?"

The private pointed to a bulge in the snake-creature's body. "It's coming from inside there."

"Sweet mother-of-all...." Charlemagne began. He pulled his field knife from its boot sheath and knelt beside the creature. He deftly inserted the knife into its body and split the creature's skin. A body, Kailee, he corrected himself, spilled out onto the ground.

Charlemagne stood and looked down at the girl, shaking his head. So much promise. Of them all, he had expected she would have come through this alive.

He closed his eyes and sighed. What a terrible waste.

"Sir?" The voice was faint but clear.

Charlemagne opened his eyes, not daring to believe. He looked down at the girl who was struggling to sit up. "What? How in the hell...."

Kailee's eyes were haunted but she tried to smile then. "Is it over, sir? Is it really you?"

Charlemagne grabbed the girl and lifted her into a bear-hug. "How is this possible, Kailee? How can you possibly be alive?"

Kailee let him hold her, mumbling into his shoulder. "After the last attack, I figured the safest place to be was inside one of the monsters. I didn't think anything else would be able to smell me there so I crawled into that dead snake-thing. It was horrible but better than the alternative."

Charlemagne held Kailee at arm's length and looked at

her before hugging her again. "It seems you were right. Let's go home. You can tell me the rest after you have had a chance to recover."

"The others...?"

"We've got them, Kailee. We will take them home."

Kailee nodded and folded up in Charlemagne's arms, finally relinquishing her consciousness. The man lifted the girl and looked over the devastation of his former troop.

Such a terrible loss of vital, important young people. He handed the girl over to a medic. "Take her through now and give her the best care possible. Understood?"

The medic nodded and took his charge through the energized portal to home.

Charlemagne waited until the last of the troopers had carried his lost kids home. A tear fell down his cheek as he left the interdicted world forever.

Time Jack

by D.J. Pitsiladis

"I've come to you today to request permission for the next phase of the project. With additional funding from the Science Council, we can proceed with human tests and be that much closer to witnessing history in person." Dr. Anabelle Gorski stared up at the group of ten individuals. Her nerves danced with anticipation and she barely stood still as they watched her with expressionless faces. She expected the group to convene in a separate room or excuse her to discuss the request, so it worried her when they remained silent and still. A part of her wondered if their minds were networked together in some way. She received her answer when one of the members finally spoke.

"We wish to thank you for coming to us with your request," the Icelandic representative, a blonde woman in her fifties, stood and said. "We found your proposal to be most interesting, as were the test results." Anabelle beamed as the woman spoke and looked to her equally excited assistant, Pamela. The glee both women felt came to an abrupt halt when the councilwoman said, "However, the council is not as convinced that your project is ready for the next phase of testing, let alone the world at large."

The room fell silent as the councilwoman's words sank in. *What just happened?* Anabelle thought before she finally found her voice. "I'm afraid I don't understand the council's decision. I provided the details of my process and listed all of the specific safeguards I employed to this point. With the information provided, I do not see how the council can dismiss my proposal without discussion, and I humbly ask for reconsideration."

"Doctor Gorski," said the Irish representative, a red-haired man of indeterminate age as he rose to his feet. "We discussed your proposal prior to your arrival, and, while you provided much information regarding your processes, there are still questions of safety and security. And there are the overlooked ethical issues."

Pamela stepped forward to join her boss and asked in a feisty tone, "What questions are there? We did everything by the book to ensure everyone's safety. And what do you mean 'ethical issues'?" The red-haired man turned to regard the assistant with a raised eyebrow. Anabelle bowed her head apologetically before she turned to her subordinate. The look she gave Pamela thanked her for speaking up and told her to step back while she dealt with the council. Pamela looked from her mentor to the collection of men and women in the gallery and nodded her head. She stepped out of the light; her face red with anger and embarrassment.

When Anabelle turned back to address the council again, she paused when the Asian representative stood and said, "While it isn't our normal practice to address questions raised by assistants, Dr. Gorski, we know they are the same questions you want answered as well. Our concerns deal specifically with the incidents that occurred in both the early stages and again in the final two rounds of testing."

"We investigated the incidents in question and discovered a minuscule deviation in the Wells generator in each case. As stated in the report, we devised a method to ensure the correct alignment and prevent any future recurrences." Anabelle stared at the woman for a full second before panning across the rest of the council members from left to right.

"The method you describe in the documentation is unorthodox and doesn't provide enough reassurance for our sake," the same woman said. "Furthermore, the fact that the test subjects were bisected in completely separate rounds of testing gives us enough cause to question the safety of your methods."

Anabelle took a deep breath, closed her eyes, and counted to ten before she replied. "As previously mentioned, the cause for those incidents has been identified, corrected, and is now a part of the pre-launch checklist in order to prevent them from occurring again." She tried to keep her frustration under control, but knew some of it came out in her voice based on the council members' expressions. "I apologize for my emotional exhibit, but I have poured every ounce of sweat and every last credit I have into this time-travel project. Without additional funding and backing from the council, the project will die and everything I've put into it will have been wasted." She fought back tears as she pleaded, "Please, do not let this project die."

The Asian representative sat down and the African representative stood up to take her place. "We do understand and appreciate the sacrifices you've made and the work you've put into this time portal. Even without our safety concerns, there are still the ethics of time travel as a whole to be considered. For example, if allowed, what would prevent someone with ill intentions from traveling into the past to facilitate changes which affect our present? What safeguards do you suggest to prevent that from occurring?" Anabelle lowered her gaze and stood silent.

After five seconds, the councilwoman returned to her seat and the British representative, a white-haired man with a refined accent, finally stood and said, "Your request for appeal has been denied for the reasons we have offered. We thank you for your efforts."

Without further comment, the remaining members of the Science Council stood up as one and filed out of the room. As custom dictated, both doctor and assistant waited until the final council member exited before they left.

Anger radiated from the women as they walked down the hallway. Once inside her hover-car, Anabelle slammed both hands against the steering yoke and a low growl escaped her throat. "I made sure every safety precaution was accounted for and followed! What more do they want?"

"Can't we take a trip into the past without obtaining their blessing?" Pamela's question took Anabelle off guard and she shot a surprised look at her excited assistant, who squirmed in her seat. "I mean, maybe we'll only be able to watch events play out like in *A Christmas Carol*." The younger woman reached a hand over to her mentor's forearm. "Maybe they'll change their minds if we prove how safe it really is."

"We only have enough fuel rods for a single jump of a minute or two," Anabelle snapped. "That's not enough time for a proper experiment, which is why we needed the council's backing. Without that, there's no project."

She let out a deep sigh. "I'm sorry. I don't mean to take my anger out on you. You've been an integral part of this whole thing, and I'm grateful to have you by my side." With a gentle squeeze of Pamela's hand, Anabelle powered up the vehicle and took off into the midday traffic.

The flight back to her lab gave Anabelle time to think about their situation. As the car navigated the skyways, she began to see if there might be other ways to get fuel for the machine. It might solve the immediate problem, but would be devastating to both their careers if they were caught. Her career was worth the risk, but Pamela's future was far too promising. Not only was she a brilliant assistant, she always knew what Anabelle needed. No matter what happened to her, Pamela didn't deserve to have her career ruined. She glanced to her right and found Pamela staring back with a sympathetic smile. "Maybe this setback will give us a chance to focus on making the processes safer."

Once the vehicle touched the ground outside of the lab, she pinched the bridge of her nose and said, "I know it's been a disappointing day, so I think it best we go home and get some rest. We can take a fresh look at everything in the morning, okay?"

A disappointed smile crossed Pamela's lips and she said with a dour tone, "Maybe you're right."

"Do you need a ride home?"

Pamela shook her head and said, "I think I'll walk around a bit. You know, to clear my head." Her lips curled up into a small, impish smile, "If I get too worked up, I always have Ben and Jerry waiting at home to cheer me up." Anabelle's eyes and mouth grew wide with shock, and the young woman's face turned a light shade of pink before she blurted out, "I meant the ice cream." The blush deepened just before she climbed out of the car.

Anabelle watched her assistant as she walked to the corner and disappeared around the corner. "She really is a great assistant," she thought. "Sure, she has her quirks, but who doesn't?

Ten minutes later, she settled down to a light dinner at home, followed by dreams of successful human time jumps. What surprised her the most was how often she pulled Pamela into a tight embrace after each test run and didn't want to let go.

Anabelle arrived at the lab in the morning with a refreshed vigor, only to have it evaporate when she found the lab door unlocked. At first she thought, "Maybe Pamela arrived early." She quickly dismissed it. The younger woman was many things, but an early riser was not one of them.

Her stomach began to flutter as she ignored her better instincts and opened the door. A part of her hoped that, if it was a burglar, they took what they wanted and left long before, but another part wanted them to be there so she could stop them from taking her equipment.

"As long as they leave the machine," she muttered as she stepped into the darkened building.

Inside, Anabelle found a middle-aged man who looked every bit out of sync with their time. His three piece suit, cape, and top hat all screamed nineteenth-century fashion. The expression he wore looked so vicious that she hesitated to draw attention to herself. When he turned and saw her, his whole demeanor changed to a gentler one.

"Who are you, and how did you get in here?" she asked, her finger ready to press the emergency call button on her wrist computer. He stepped toward her, but stopped when she lifted her wrist and finger.

"Look, she said. "I'm tired and feel rather dejected after yesterday, so why don't we make a deal? Tell me what you're doing in my lab or I call the police." The doctor took a step forward with her hands in view and a serious expression on her face. "Who do you want to deal with more?"

"My presence in your laboratory is as much a mystery to me, madam. Rest assured, the moment I'm apprised of the reason, I shall convey the information to you." The man spoke with a crisp British accent, but not the New British Empire. His manner of speech was more articulate with clear enunciation. "John J. Bonner," he said, and offered a flourished bow only royalty used.

"The clock is still ticking, Mr. Bonner. You now have ten seconds to answer my question." Despite her nervousness, Anabelle felt excitement well up inside her and it took a lot to push her excitement down.

"He's here because I brought him," a woman's voice said from behind the man. Anabelle turned and found an excited Pamela as she crossed the floor in a white lab coat, a guilty smirk plastered on her face.

Anabelle's eyes shifted from Pamela to Mr. Bonner and back. "No," she said in disbelief. "Tell me you didn't use the machine, not after what I told you yesterday. You're so..."

Pamela cut off Anabelle's admonishment mid-sentence when she wrapped her arms around her neck and pulled her into a kiss. The older woman's eyes widened in shock for a couple of seconds before she regained her composure and pushed her protégé away. With the back of her hand pressed against her mouth, Anabelle tried to process what happened and found it difficult to do.

"Disgusting," Mr. Bonner exclaimed with a grimace that broke the nervous silence.

Both women looked at him, and Anabelle saw the glint of danger in his eyes again. As quickly as it appeared, the look vanished behind his aristocratic air. Anabelle looked at her excited assistant, lowered her hand, and said, "My office. Now!"

Pamela's joy-filled grin fell. With a last pained look, the young woman headed to the small office she had emerged from moments ago.

Meanwhile, Anabelle turned to their guest and said, "Please excuse us for a moment or two. My assistant and I need to discuss our plans to return you home. Please, make yourself comfortable."

Mr. Bonner nodded, but the look on his face conveyed his displeasure with the situation. She flashed what she hoped was a reassuring smile and walked to her office.

Once inside the room, she darkened the glass. It gave them privacy to talk without losing sight of Mr. Bonner. She took the few seconds it took for the glass to change to gain her composure, and asked in a calm voice, "Can you tell me where, or should I ask when, that man came from?"

Pamela looked at her feet like a child caught misbehaving. "I don't know," she said without looking up. "I mean, I punched in some numbers, turned the machine on, and pulled the nearest person through." She looked up with a weak smile and said, "I thought we could check what they were once we get more fuel cells."

"Excuse me?" Anabelle asked with wide eyes. "What do you mean 'once we get more fuel cells'? If you just plucked the first person you saw, there should be just enough to send him back through." She waited for Pamela to answer. Her assistant remained silent. "You used up all of our fuel to pull that man through, didn't you?" The older woman felt her heart leap into her throat when her assistant nodded. Anabelle fought the urge to smack the other woman, but managed to let her mind wrest control from her emotions. "Tell me exactly what happened, and don't leave anything out."

Pamela stood silent for a good minute before she said in a

soft voice, "I was so excited, I forgot to turn the machine off after I pulled Mr. Bonner through. Before I realized it, the cells ran dry and the portal closed."

"Please don't be mad. I did it to show those shortsighted hive minds how wrong they are; that the portal isn't dangerous. I didn't want you to damage your reputation, and I don't have one to damage yet." The younger woman surprised Anabelle when she dropped to her knees, threw her arms around her mentor's waist, and buried her face against the woman's stomach. "Please don't hate me," she sobbed. "I did it for you, all for you."

Surprised by the confession, Anabelle stroked Pamela's head and said, "It'll be okay. We'll fix this. Shh." When the tears finished, the scientist helped her up and offered a tissue. *We have got a lot to talk about when this is over*, she thought as she walked to her desk.

"Look, I need to contact some people and find out how we can get more cells without the council finding out what happened. I need you to keep an eye on Mr. Bonner and make sure he doesn't leave this building."

Pamela took a step toward the desk and looked ready to argue.

Without looking up, Anabelle said, "We need to keep his exposure to our time minimal. The last thing we need is for him to learn something from our present before we get him home."

There was a pregnant pause before Anabelle said, "I know you meant well. When this is over, you and I are going to sit down and talk about our relationship, both the working one and this..." She paused for a second while she tried to wrap her mind around the rest of it."... other thing." She smiled at Pamela, who responded with a shy little smirk of her own. She felt guilty about raising the young woman's hopes, but needed her to focus on the problem at hand.

It took all day, but Anabelle managed to find a source willing to provide the necessary fuel cells. She was exhausted and frustrated at the favors she needed to promise in exchange for them. "Now, we just need to entertain our guest until they're delivered," she thought.

When she opened the office door to tell Pamela the good news, Anabelle frowned. Save for the light from the doorway behind her and a couple of computer monitors, the entire lab was cloaked in darkness.

"Hello?" she called out. "Is anyone here?" Her frown deepened when only her echo answered and she reached for the light panel to her right. "I told her to keep him here," she thought. "She's going to ruin everything before it even gets fixed."

A quick glance at one of the computers revealed their project notes on the time portal. Additional notes written in Pamela's hand lay on the desk. After a quick read-through, she was reminded of how smart she really was. *Add "holding back for so long" to the discussion list*, she thought.

With a satisfied smile, she turned to the second monitor and read the screen. Her upturned lips slowly drooped into a frown when she saw it was a Wikipedia article on Jack the Ripper. She got a bad feeling in the pit of her stomach. She checked the browser's history, only to find it empty. "Okay, she didn't want me to know she shared some information with him, but why leave this page up?"

On a whim, Anabelle went to the time portal's controls and prayed for enough power to find out the coordinates Pamela used. The seconds it took to boot up the system stretched on for an unsettling amount of time. When the system finished loading, the screen read "London, England: 11-09-1888" before it shut down. A heaviness settled in her stomach and she asked through gritted teeth, "What part of London did that idiot go to?"

"White Chapel," a voice said from behind her. She spun around and found Mr. Bonner with his arms behind his back. "I know what you're thinking." He stepped forward and made exaggerated gestures with his left hand. "Is it him? Is it really him?" He took another step and bowed without breaking eye contact, "Allow me to introduce myself." He flashed an evil grin and said, "Jack the Ripper at your service." When he straightened, the cloak fell from his shoulders to reveal a unique knife.

Anabelle pulled a desk chair between them and kept it ready in case he rushed her. "What did you do with Pamela?" Jack grinned and wiggled the knife in front of his face. Her eyes focused on the metal blade, she shoved the chair at him and turned to run. After only a few steps, she tripped and landed hard on the floor. When she turned to find out where the serial killer was, her eyes met Pamela's dead eyes.

"She loved you, you know," he said with a giggle that made Anabelle's skin crawl while he knelt behind Pamela's head and brushed the knife against her hair.

"You were more than just a mentor or a friend to her. I've seen true love like that, you know, just never between two women." Jack pulled Pamela's hair away from her neck to reveal a deep, ragged wound.

"My life's purpose is to remove undesirables from the population like a surgeon with a scalpel." He lowered the hair and closed her eyes. "I was in the middle of such a hunt when she dragged me into that glowing hole." He motioned vaguely in the direction of the machine with his knife, "I thought it the doorway to hell at first; that maybe I misunderstood my calling and faced eternal damnation for it. But then I learned how sinful the world has become, and then I saw the two of you. The moment her lips touched yours, I knew this time and place needed me." He stood and kicked the lifeless body out of the way with his foot. "Now that you arranged for fuel and I have the notes on how to run your machine, I can go wherever and whenever I'm needed to prevent this future and form it into a world God will feel proud of."

Anabelle crawled away on her elbows as he advanced. She tried to get to her feet, only to feel his foot smash into her tail-bone and shove her down. He held her there until his other boot slammed into her ribs. She curled into a ball and gasped for air. When the first breath entered, Jack flipped her over and placed his knees on her shoulders. The scientist felt the blade slide across her neck, severing vocal cords, arteries, and veins in one surprising movement. The pool of blood grew under her as Jack laughed and whispered in her ear, "Let the reign of the Ripper begin anew."

Author Biographies

Kevin Wohler is a fantasy / science fiction short story writer and novelist. He lives in Lawrence, Kansas, with his wife, author R.L. Naquin. He has a grown daughter and son, and a growing collection of LEGO sets. His short story "Ultimatums: Giving Up the Element of Surprise" was featured in the 2013 anthology *A Method to the Madness: A Guide to the Super Evil*. He plans to publish the first novel in his Alchemist series in 2015.

Philip Carroll is an old man, getting older all the time. While he has been a storyteller most of his life, he has spent the last seven years honing the skills of putting those stories into recorded words on paper, electronic media, and audio.

He has two novels recently released as e-books on Amazon.com and print on demand through Create Space. He has books at Podiobooks.com in serialized audio, an ongoing podcast on iTunes, and other serialized fiction at Channillo.com.

When not working as a certified orthotist, he spends his time with his wife and children, writing, and playing the piano.

He can be contacted at norvaljoe@gmail.com

Charlie Brown is a writer and filmmaker from New Orleans. He currently lives in Los Angeles, where he recently received his master's in professional writing from the University of Southern California and also runs Lucky Mojo Press and Mojotooth Productions. He has made two feature films: *Angels Die Slowly* and *Never a Dull Moment: 20 Years of the*

Rebirth Brass Band. His fiction has appeared in Oddville Press, Writing Disorder, Jersey Devil Press, The Menacing Hedge, Aethlon, and what?? Magazine.

When not listening to the voices inside his head, **J.R. Murdock** spends time with his wife and his favorite daughter (yes, there is only one daughter – that's why she's his favorite). They reside in sunny San Diego, which is about as close to paradise as you can get and still be in a big city.

Christopher Hite is the oldest of 10 kids. His dad infected him with the writing bug when he was eleven with his podcast *Great Hites*. He enjoys watching and reading *Star Trek*, running, biking, and of course, writing. Christopher lives somewhere in the middle of nowhere, raises sheep and chickens, and enjoys the country air.

Dan Absalonson first started writing stories in elementary school, where he and a friend would skip lunch and recess once a month to eat in the library while hearing all about the new books on the shelves. His love for reading, as well as visual art and music, has now extended into creating his own fiction. He works as a digital artist and lives in the state of Washington with his beautiful family of five. A huge fan of audio books, Dan podcasts all of his stories for free. You can find many free and a couple cheap e-books of his stories at all the popular online retailers. Dan loves podcasting his fiction, but is involved in a few other podcasts as well.

Julayne Hughes is a freelance writer and editor with over 20 years' experience in that field. Her science fiction short story

"Solara Nova" was published in *FlagShip* magazine; two fantasy shorts, "The Ghost of Edinburgh Castle" and "The Caprine Catastrope," were featured on the *Every Photo Tells . . .* podcast; and her flash fiction has appeared on *The Melting Potcast.*

On the editing side, Julayne has done everything from books of poetry to full-length novels for a variety of small publishers and independent authors. Some of her recent work has included *The Way of the Gun: A Bushido Western Anthology* compiled by Scott Roche, *The Starter* by Scott Sigler, and *Smoke Stories: Tales of a Volunteer Firefighter* by Mike Davis. She has also edited the work of her husband, podcaster Keith Hughes (*Borrowed Time, Stolen Time*, and *The Guerrilla Poet*).

When Julayne is not writing and editing, she plays piano and teaches music classes at a local private college. She lives in southeastern Michigan with her husband, their grown daughter, and a gray-and-white cat named Gandalf.

Julayne has a neglected blog at http:// pianoeditor.blogspot.com and can be found on Facebook and Twitter as pianoeditor.

Jeff Hite, A.K.A. The Dark Lord Hite, A.K.A. Dr. Evil-n-Carnate, A.K.A. Steve Wolencheck, current occupant of cubical 3257J, affectionately referred to as "that jerk who eats lunch in his cubicle even though we have a lunch room and he really should eat there," is, first and foremost, a husband and father. He and his wife and their ten minions er...children, live in their orbiting space station. No, that burned up in the atmosphere last year. They live in their undersea lab. No, that is not right either, it fell to crush depth three months ago. Well, wherever they live, that is where you can find them.

By day he is an IT professional and by night, when he and his partner in crime, Alex the 486 Beowulf Super cluster are not trying to take over the world, they run the "sheep dating service," also known as sheep breeding, for the local farming cooperative. When he can fit it in, he writes short fiction about the fantastic, is an assistant editor and head slush reader with the *Cast Of Wonders*podcast, and an assistant audio producer for the podcast *Get Published*.

He and his alter ego Michell Plested are co-editors of *A Method to the Madness: A Guide to the Super Evil* and he is the author of several short stories, which you can find at his website http://jeffreyhite.com

He and his wife homeschool their minions, er...kids, and teach NFP to anyone who will listen. The rest of his life is devoted to his first love, his family, their chickens, sheep, dogs, and now to appease the cat owners, one of those as well.

Michell (Mike) Plested is an author, editor, blogger, closet superhero (not to mention sock herder and cat wrangler) and podcaster living in Calgary, Alberta, Canada. He is the host of several podcasts including the writing podcast, *Get Published* (2009, 2011, 2013 and 2014 Parsec Finalist).

His debut novel, *Mik Murdoch: Boy Superhero* was shortlisted for the Prix Aurora Award for Best YA Novel, and its sequel, *Mik Murdoch: The Power Within* was launched at When Words Collide 2014. He has stories and several books coming out this year (2015) including *Scouts of the Apocalypse* (May), and a collaborative steampunk work, *Jack Kane & the Statue of Liberty* (June).

He can be contacted at author@michellplested.com.

D.J. Pitsiladis is a writer of horror, science fiction, and thrillers. When not working a day job or creating fiction, he

spends time with his fiancée, children, dogs, and a cat he calls his "little muse." You can catch more of his work and reviews on his *Casa de Pitsiladis* blog (http://dpitsiladis.wordpress.com) and on HorrorAddicts.net.

OTHER EVIL ALTER EGO PRESS BOOKS

Scouts of the Apocalypse: Zombie Plague
By Michell Plested

ISBN: 978-0-9947266-2-9 (paperback)
ISBN: 978-0-9947266-3-6 (digital eBook)

The Fountain
By Suzy Vadori

ISBN 978-0-9947266-4-3 (paperback.).
ISBN 978-0-9947266-5-0 (digital eBook)

www.ingramcontent.com/pod-product-compliance
Lightning Source LLC
Chambersburg PA
CBHW071257130626
46556CB00003B/1347